GIO
&
GRACE

WILLOW WINTERS &
B.B. HAMEL
WALL STREET JOURNAL & USA TODAY BESTSELLING AUTHOR

From USA Today bestselling Author Willow Winters and B. B. Hamel comes a darker emotionally-gripping, standalone, romantic suspense.

I should have known that one day
I'd be at the mercy of a monster.
And all I am is the daughter of his enemy.

I was stolen and gifted to him.
A dominating, brutal and a cold hearted killer.
My pleas fall on deaf ears as I stay trapped and held hostage to his will.
He could do anything he wanted with me.
And I know what it is he's looking for.

He can't hide the desire in his gaze.
The flicker of heat between us is something I can't deny either.
And as the days grow colder, I'm finding it harder to resist.

With each gentle touch and act of kindness that lures me closer to him, I'm finding it impossible to remember why I should fight this.

FORSAKEN

PROLOGUE

GRACE

Beaten. Broken. Used as a bargaining chip. I've been through hell. *He* can't do anything that hasn't already been done to me. Except show me tenderness, kindness... pleasure. And he has. In a way I didn't know I needed.

Goosebumps travel down my arms as I hear his heavy footsteps echoing in the hall. My steady heartbeat quickens.

He's come back for me. I'm almost surprised by the excitement I feel. The rush of adrenaline, and the anticipation of hearing the click of the lock on the door. *Almost.*

My fingers wrap around the thin bars as he enters. My captor. I could come out, I could let him have me. I know Gio wants me, and I'd be a liar if I said I didn't want him, too. His hard ripped body and the heat in his eyes tempt me to come out of my cage. The door's never locked, so l could easily leave. But l'm safe here.

He said he won't touch me, and he's held firm to his promise. So long as l stay inside of the cage, l'm protected. But l want to come out. l want his praise. *I've grown addicted to it.* His very presence is a drug.

l'm desperate for him, and he knows it. l want to resist. l want to hold out against whatever sickness is taking me over. But l can't. He's too much. *He's everything.*

There's a darkness inside of him, a dangerous beast. l know what he's capable of, but when he's with me, there's a sense of calm about him. Maybe l'm naive to think l affect him as much as he does me, but the very thought that l do makes me feel powerful.

The sound of the door creaking open and his broad shoulders filling up the doorway make my lips part, and a moan of lust escapes my throat. My nipples harden, and my clit throbs with need. He's done this to me. He's trained me to react like this. l know it's the truth, but l can't deny l enjoy it.

"My princess," he says and his voice is rough and deep. It reminds me of how he groaned when he first took me. It's the sexiest fucking sound l've ever heard. He's just as obsessed with me as l am with him. It's only fair.

l lick my lips and shift on my knees, facing him and leaning forward. l don't leave the safety of the cage though. l want him to lure me out. Is that so wrong?

"I miss you," he whispers, crouching in front of the cage, his fingers curling above mine around the bars. My heart thumps hard in my chest, and my body begs me to just reach out. To climb into his lap and let him hold me. It's my choice. But the only choice I've been given.

I've never felt so loved before. Even if it's an illusion and nothing more.

But that doesn't stop me from craving it.

"Tell me you missed me," e commands, and my mouth parts on its own. The words are there, right on the tip of my tongue. I flirt with the idea of saying them, but I close my lips shut tight

He tilts his head, narrowing his eyes and tsking me for disobeying him. Again I shift on my knees, questioning my decision to keep fighting him.

His expression softens as he sits in front of me, lowering himself as my eyes look down at him. I settle onto the floor of the cage across from him. Merely inches away, but so much farther than that all the same.

"I know you did." As he says the words, his dark eyes heat and a cocky grin plays at his lips.

I can't help my eyes widening and a smile slowly slipping across my lips. I wish I could hide it, but I can't hide anything from him. Not anymore.

I don't want to go back to the way things were. I know it's

wrong, but I had nothing before him. I'm drunk on his touch, his words. He's everything I could possibly need. He's shown me that.

I may be broken. But I'm *his.*

CHAPTER 1

GIO
ONE MONTH BEFORE

The bright red rubber ball squeaks as I release it, watching it sail far across my yard. Duke, my loyal black lab, turns and chases the ball as fast as he can, tearing up the grass in pursuit.

I smile to myself, looking out across the property. I like the seclusion and privacy of living outside of the city, and I was able to construct a home with everything I could need. I bought the place more for the land than for anything else. I'd be happy living in a fucking trailer if it meant I could do whatever I damn well please, but fortunately I get paid a lot of money to do what I do.

"You know we can't turn this down."

I glance at my father at the sound of his voice. He stands

impatiently against a nearby tree, puffing one of the short, dark cigars he prefers. His receding white hair makes him look ten years older than he is. He's wearing his usual outfit, a blue dress shirt tucked into jeans with a brown work jacket over top and oversized brown boots that are nearly falling apart. He looks like a construction worker, or something blue collar like that.

He sure as hell works with his hands, but he's no fucking construction worker.

"You know that if we do it, the consequences could be extensive," I answer, feeling a chill run down my shoulders.

Duke grabs the ball and heads back, his tail held high in the air. My father huffs, shaking his head and then inhales deeply, looking past me.

His voice is low as he responds, "I understand your concerns, but this is beyond us."

"Exactly. It's too big to control," I answer, not bothering to look at him.

"Control?" He laughs. "There's no control in our line of work."

"Maybe the way you operate. But that's not how I do things."

He pushes off the tree and walks toward me just as Duke drops the ball at my feet. I pick it up and launch it again, sending the dog running. The smell of the cigar gets stronger as he walks closer.

"Listen, son. You know how much this means to me."

Guilt threatens to take over. The only man I owe shit to

is my father. But he's falling for a trap. They'll never give him what he wants. "I know what it *could* mean, at least."

"We've been outsiders our whole fucking lives." His voice rises, letting his emotions come through.

"I know," I say, jaw tense.

"They think we're garbage and trash," he says, nearly spitting the words. "But this is our chance to show them that we're dependable. That we belong."

I grunt and watch the dog sprint off in the distance. My father's right, even though his motives are pretty fucking skewed. He's lived his entire life on the outskirts of the Romano *familia*, wishing he could be a part of them, but unable to join. He's only half Italian; his disgraced father ran off and fucked some Irish girl years and years ago. It doesn't matter to me, but my father never got over the fact that his full Italian Romano cousins were allowed into the *familia*, while he was kept at a distance.

That's probably why my father entered into this profession and trained me to work alongside him. Being hitmen means we're allowed to exist on the fringe of the *familia*. We've even earned some respect, though fear may be the better word for it. Over the years my father gathered a particular set of skills and passed them down to me, continuing the family tradition.

I don't give a shit about my inbred, shitheel cousins. I could kill them one by one if I wanted and never lose a wink of sleep. Blood means nothing to me.

I don't give a fuck about the *familia* like my father does. He has this chip on his shoulder and acts like all of our problems are due to the *familia* rejecting him. He can't see past his own petty need to be accepted by them.

Being an outsider suits me. I like my life outside of the city, and outside of the *familia*. I take their money and do their jobs because that's the life I know, but I don't want to be a part of their politics and their bullshit.

Taking this job offer though would destroy any semblance of outsider status and shove us right into the high-stakes world of mafia power plays. I don't fucking want that. I'm not interested.

"Think of the money," he tries to persuade me. "I know you don't care about the *familia* like I do." There's a hint of bitterness in his tone, and it makes my body tense. "But think of the money they're offering."

He has a good point. They're offering to pay us triple our normal rate, which is significant already. The target is difficult to get to and very important, but the money is absurdly good.

A man could possibly retire with that kind of cash.

"If we do this, our lives will change," I say, meeting his cold gaze.

"Exactly." My father smiles, his yellowed teeth showing for only a moment before he takes another puff of his cigar.

I shake my head. "You see it as a good thing, but to me this would destroy everything we've built."

His boots are heavy and his steps quick as he tosses the

cigar aside. He walks up to me and suddenly grabs my jacket by the collar, bunching the fabric up in his fists. My hands clench into fists, but I wait. I'm used to this. I grew up with it.

I can see the anger in his eyes, the intense fury that dwells deep inside. It's a darkness that eats away at him, and I know that he drinks more than he should to try and keep it at bay.

I have the same darkness inside of me. It comes out in different ways, but it's there, slowly rotting me from the inside. I hate my father in this moment because I see myself in him, and it disgusts me. My knuckles go white and adrenaline pumps hard in my blood, but I keep it down, waiting for him to get out whatever's on his mind.

He better do it quick, 'cause I don't have time for this shit.

"You can't fuck this up for me," he growls. His face is close to mine, but I don't move. I don't give him the opportunity to see me weak. "The *familia*'s denied me for far too long. This is our chance to make things right for our family."

Duke returns without the ball and growls at my father. It's low and rough, from somewhere deep down in his throat.

"I'd let me go if I were you," I say softly, cocking a brow and looking my father in the eye. Duke doesn't have the type of control I do. But he'll always wait for my command.

"What, you gonna send that fucking dog after me?" He scoffs, but it's quick and panic is barely hidden beneath it.

"No," I say, staring him down. "You know I don't need his help."

There's a strained moment between us. I can see my father doing the math in his head, wondering if he could take me in a fair fight now that I'm older. We've come close to fighting in the past, though we've never actually traded blows. But we both know I have youth and experience on my side, and so he slowly releases me and takes a deep breath.

He picks up the cigar he dropped on the ground and takes a long puff, looking away as he walks back to the oak tree, ignoring everything that just happened. That's what he does. Thickheaded, thin-skinned and hot-tempered. That's the Romano in him.

I walk across the yard and bend down, picking up the ball Duke left, and throw it. Duke darts after it as if nothing happened.

"Just think about it," he finally says, forcing me to look over my shoulder and face him. "If we kill this fucker, we can be rolling in it for a long time."

"If we kill this fucker, we can start a war." I bite out my words. That's the real reason I don't want in on this.

He shrugs, rubbing out his cigar on the tree and letting out a deep exhalation of smoke. "Let's just wait and see what they have to say." He glances at me, a look of determination on his face, and then heads off back toward his truck.

I don't watch him go. I know he's pissed, and I understand that. Fuck, I can't even blame him, not really. Joining the *familia* is his lifelong dream, and if someone got in the way of what I wanted, well, I'd fucking kill them.

Too bad the old bastard needs me. The sound of his truck starting fills the chilly air as Duke comes back to me.

I'm his rightful successor. He's getting old, too old to go on hits, and for the last two years I've been taking on more and more of the load. In fact, he hasn't actually killed in nearly six months, which is strange for a man who makes his living in death.

He raised me to be a killer and to be the fucking best at what I do. From a young age I remember going to shooting ranges, and practicing knife skills. My childhood was almost exclusively learning to fight, learning to stalk, and learning how to kill efficiently and quietly. My father trained me to be a hitman, and I quickly found out that I was damn good at it.

And I like it. I like tracking down my victims and taking their lives. They all deserve it. They have it coming to them. As far as I'm concerned, I'm doing the world a favor. I like the power and respect I get for being a skilled and in-demand assassin. Nobody fucks with me because they know who I am, and what I'm capable of. No one can push me around. They wouldn't fucking dare.

But I can't deny that it fucked me up. That it changed me. I can remember the way I was back when I was still a kid, back before killing became my life. The darkness wasn't there back then. I wasn't born with it. It was created.

As I pitch the ball across the yard again, I remember the day my father brought me completely into this life and forced me to kill a man for the first time.

My father stands over me in the cellar. My breath comes in ragged, short gasps.

"Don't be a pussy," he says to me, his voice barely above a whisper as he grips my shoulders. "You fucking afraid?"

"No," I say, but I'm lying. I'm terrified. I'm ten years old and I've never seen a man die before. Not in real life.

The old man's tied to a chair with a gag in his mouth, muffling his screams and pleas. I don't know him. His eyes are wide and brown. His hair is receding and he's probably fifty years old, but I didn't really know that back then. I was just a kid. I didn't know anything.

"What did he do?" I ask tentatively, and my voice cracks. My heart is beating so loudly I can hardly hear anything else.

My father whirls on me. "You fucking know not to ask questions." The anger in his voice makes me flinch. Ever since Mom died, it's been different between us. He takes his rage out on me. It's my fault.

"I know," I say, looking away from him. I expect him to hit me, and I wait for it... but he doesn't. My body is so hot. I feel like I can't even breathe.

"It doesn't matter what he did. All that matters is we get paid. These guys, they're all shit. You have to understand that." The man screams again behind his gag, but whatever he's saying is dampened. I wish I knew.

"I understand." I look at the man as my father walks over

to him. He takes the man by what hair he has left and pulls his head back.

"Look at him, Gio," my father says. "Look at this man. Are you looking?"

"Yes, father," I say, staring at the man.

"This is our prey. He's our victim. He's nothing." My father releases him. "Are you a fucking pussy?"

"No," I say and step toward the man. My nerves are shaken, but I have to do this.

"Good. Very good, Gio."

The man struggles and tries to say something. He's panicking and trying to move again like he knows it's his last chance. My father backhands him across the face and his head droops. He's dazed, but not unconscious.

"What now?" I ask my father. I've been training for this since I was very young. I know how to shoot and how to fight and how to hunt, but this is the first time my father is making me watch.

Except watching isn't what he has planned. He holds his gun out to me, grip first. "Take it," he says.

I stare at him, shocked. "Why?" I ask.

"Do as I say."

Afraid, I take the gun. I expect him to hit me again for not following orders right away, but he doesn't. My hands shake.

I know something irreversible is happening. But I don't understand what, not yet.

"Press it against his head," my father orders.

I stand so close to the man I can feel the heat and desperation roiling off of him. His eyes are wide and pleading, staring at me, practically looking through me. He squirms against the restraints. I press the gun against his head. My throat is so tight, I can't swallow. I watch as the man begins to cry, deep heaving sobs. I hold the gun there, the cold steel feeling hotter as my hand starts to sweat, and I look at my father.

"Look back at him," my father commands. I try to swallow again, but I fail miserably. I stare at the man, but only at his temple where the gun is pointed. I can't look him in the eyes. "Are you ready, Gio?"

It comes to me in that moment, what my father wants. It's the reason he's not hitting me. Because he knows I'm about to do something important. I don't want to though. I don't want this. I hold the gun tightly, then grip it with two hands.

"I- I-" I stammer. I can't do this. I'm not like him.

"You will do it, or I'll untie him and let him beat you to death," my father sneers. My blood runs cold, and I finally swallow the spiked lump that has formed in my throat.

"I'm ready," I say in a voice I don't recognize.

Ten years old. My father puts a hand on my shoulder. His fingers dig in as he squeezes.

"Do it," he says.

I pull the trigger without thinking anything more. Bang! The man's skull explodes in a shower of blood. The sound, the feel, and the sight of the man, hung over and limp in the chair

haunted me for years. But not the next man, or the next that my
father had me kill. I don't even remember them.

I hate him for what he made me, but at the same time, I'm
also glad for what he made me. I can take lives so easily now.
They mean nothing to me. That first time was difficult, but it
was also surprisingly easy.

One pull of the trigger, and it all ends. I'm safe, and
the world is rid of a man who needed to die. The darkness
inside of me needs this. It craves the rush and the thrill of a
hunt and a kill, and if I go too long without a job I find that
darkness coming up to the surface in the form of memories.
Too much of my past still haunts me. I just need to focus on
the present. *On the next kill.*

Duke returns with the ball. I crouch down and pat his
shoulder, just now noticing how the sky has darkened and
the air has turned bitter cold. "Good boy," I say softly. I relax
as Duke nudges me, bringing me back to the present. "Next
time, just rip off his nuts."

Duke licks my hand as I grin, pick up the ball, and throw
it. He barks as he runs off, leaving me alone with the dilemma
at hand.

My father wants me to at least hear what they have to say,
and I can do that. I'll listen, because I owe him that much.
But I can't imagine how they could change my mind on this
one. Not when this hit could spark the largest mafia war in
the history of the whole fucking city.

CHAPTER 2

GRACE

Knock, knock. The hard pounding on my bedroom door forces my eyes open. I don't shake or shudder, and I don't flinch when the door opens without a response from me. I'm used to it now. My breathing comes in carefully, each movement calculated.

The door creaks and then shuts with a loud bang as I rise and blink the sleep from my eyes. I don't know how long I've been asleep, but it doesn't matter. It's not like I have anything else to do, or anywhere to go.

I restrain myself from stretching and sit up on the edge of my bed, my hands clasped in my lap as I watch my father walk toward me. I'm used to this, but my heart still races with fear.

Everything else I can control, but not my heart. No matter how much I want it to remain calm, it always beats harder and tries to escape up my throat whenever he comes to get me. I never know what to expect, but I know how to behave. I've learned the hard way, but now I know how to survive. That's all I do... *survive.*

If I was a boy, it wouldn't be like this. But I'm a *disappointment.* A reminder of my mother, and how she betrayed him. That's all I am. He never fails to make sure I know it.

"You need to do something for me," he says in a lowered voice. It holds the edge of a threat when he talks to me. It's always there, like he's waiting for me to give him a reason to strike me. Unless Uncle Toni's in the room. Just the thought of my godfather makes my heart calm slightly. He can't kill me with my uncle still around. My mother, yes, but not me. Uncle Toni would never allow it.

My father may be the Don of the Rossi *familia*, but everyone knows my uncle Toni calls the shots. They all look to him with respect, and they're loyal to him... not to my father. The very thought almost wills me to smile, but I'm not that foolish.

"The Romanos are up to something." I stare straight ahead, my neck stiff as he talks.

He crosses the room, moving to my window and then back toward me. "They've been circling our territory and looking for something." He continues talking without waiting for a response. He doesn't need one from me. We both know that.

I bow my head and keep my eyes down as he paces the floor in front of me. His suit pants swish as he walks and make up the only background noise. He usually doesn't talk *business* around me. He says it's not for women, and I honestly prefer to be left out of it. My fingers dig into the comforter as he speaks, knowing something terrible is going to happen. I don't want to know, but for him to be telling me these things... it's not good. "I don't like it, and you're going to fix this," he practically hisses, turning harshly in his spot and staring at me. I look up to meet his gaze, but only to keep him from touching me. My eyes meet his as I nod my head like I'm supposed to, but inside I'm screaming.

"The Romanos have been hanging around our restaurant; they're on our turf, looking for trouble." His pale blue eyes piercing into mine hold me hostage as my lungs pause their movements. "You're going out there as bait."

I don't react, but he still holds up his pointer and lowers his voice as if I've disobeyed him. Sometimes I can't prevent him from beating me, but it's best not to react, so I'm still as he says, "You don't have a choice. You're going to get us the information we need, and we'll get you out."

For a moment I question if he'll really come save me, or if the Romanos will get to keep me. I'm not sure it matters much. Although at least here I know what to expect. I rely on the comfort of familiarity. I search my father's face for answers, for reassurance. But there's nothing there. Only emptiness in his dark eyes.

"They're going to take you. You need to trust me and stay focused. Listen to what they say and when I come to get you, you'll tell me everything."

I'm numb to his words. It wouldn't be the first time he's used me for his own plans. I nod my head once, although I don't speak. He doesn't like it when I talk.

My heart leaps in my chest as he grips my chin in his hand and rips my head to the side.

"Answer me!" he screams at me. His stale breath fills my lungs as I heave in a frightened breath. After all these years I still cower. Maybe there's a part of me that isn't dead yet.

"Yes, father. I'll listen to everything." My throat feels so tight, but the words come out calmly. "I'll tell you everything." My blood runs cold. I ignore the voices arguing inside of me. One is telling me to run, and the other is telling me to fight back. Those voices are useless. *They both get me nothing but beatings.* I'm smarter than that now. It's not about fear, only survival.

"Good," he says as he releases me, and I fall back into place as he talks to me. "We'll drop you off at the restaurant, and you can walk back home. They've been scouting every day in the evening, so it shouldn't take more than a day or two before they get confident and take you."

I half expect him to tell me not to worry, but I don't hold my breath. I should be worried, and I am. More than that, he doesn't give a fuck if I live or die. Maybe he really needs the information, or maybe he's just looking to finally get rid of me.

I think about what he's asking, and hope rises in my chest.

I'll be alone. For the first time since I can remember, I'll be alone. I try to hide the excitement rising in me. *The hope.*

Maybe this will be my chance to run. I don't want to be the Rossi mafia princess anymore. I don't want to be a pawn in my father's games and get married off to whoever he wants to make alliances with. Although there's a faint hope that I can run and disappear, it's only barely there. It's faded to a mere whisper of what it used to be.

I've tried before to run, and failed. I have the scars to prove it's not possible to outrun the Rossis.

"Do you understand, Grace?" my father asks, practically spitting out my name like a curse.

"Yes, father." My eyes fall to the floor. It's better not to look him in the eyes, especially when I feel like this... when I feel hopeful. "Whatever you need me to do."

"Good." He turns and walks to the door with heavy steps, speaking without looking at me. "Get yourself dressed. We're leaving soon."

My hands ball into fists as the door closes, and my breathing comes in ragged pants. The facade leaves me quickly. I hate him. With everything in my being, I hate him. I rise from the bed and look out my window. It's nailed shut from the outside to keep me from jumping.

Outside, it's dark and grey with clouds covering nearly every inch of the visible sky. It reflects everything that I feel.

I walk to my dresser, my eyes darting to the door. Inside the top drawer, I dig under the pile of shirts and pick up a small bag of heroin. I wrap my fingers around it tightly. I've never done the drug, or any others for that matter. I stole it. I've collected a few baggies over time, and I know I have enough to easily overdose now.

I've been thinking about suicide for a while, but I haven't had the courage to end it. I don't want to die; I just don't want to live *this* life anymore. There's a difference. I stare at the heroin, feeling every emotion wash over me. I knew one day I'd need it.

I would be a fool not to take the heroin with me. I need a way out in case my father doesn't come for me and leaves me there. In case that fate is worse than this. I open the drawer containing my underwear and select my favorite push-up bra. Quickly, I slide the packet into one of the pockets containing the padded inserts. I just hope that whoever takes me won't search my clothing too closely, but in my experience the perverts I've been exposed to care more about seeing a woman naked than her lingerie.

But hopefully it won't even come close to that. He's giving me a chance to run. An opportunity I've prayed for.

Maybe God was listening. Maybe I'll be free soon.

If not, if I can't get away from my father, if I can't get away from the Romanos... at least I'll have a way out.

CHAPTER 3

GRACE

The hushed sounds of the restaurant and my own blood pumping in my ears are the only things I can hear. My eyes flicker to the bay window at the front as the bells at the entrance jingle, and another member of the *familia* walks through the glass double doors.

The restaurant is so quaint and gives off a family-friendly feel. The dark green cloth table linens and plaid curtains on the windows make this place look like the quintessential Italian restaurant. Even the soft music playing over the speakers gives an air of comfort.

It's all bullshit. It's a front, and the entire city knows it. I glance up and across the room at my father, seated at the table farthest from me as he talks animatedly to someone I haven't met. He leans back as he laughs, the sound bellowing from his stomach. He looks jovial. That's fake, too. *Or is it?* Maybe he's happy that I'll be gone soon. I still don't know his intentions, but I don't care. I'm grateful. Scared shitless and trying to control my emotions, but grateful.

The bells chime again, and I whip my head up to see another man walk through the doors. The restaurant is closed tonight. But that doesn't mean anything.

I can feel their eyes on me. Everyone's looking at me as they talk in indistinct voices. I'm not supposed to be here. Some are confused by my presence. Others are visibly anxious. A man across from me doesn't bother to look away when I meet his eyes. His fingertips tap repeatedly on the wooden table. He clears his throat and breaks my gaze, running the back of his hand across his mouth and yelling out for someone named Joey to grab him a beer.

Maybe they all don't know what's going on, but some do.

I can't help but look over my shoulder one more time, searching for Uncle Toni. I don't know anyone in here other than my father. I think that may have been an intentional play by him. No one's talked to me, but I have no intention of talking to them either.

Two firm hands grip my shoulders as I turn in my seat. I nearly yell out from the sudden touch, but the sight of my father's cold eyes keeps me quiet. His fingers dig into my skin, and I wonder if the men can tell it hurts. If they do know, they don't show it. They don't try to stop him.

"Now." He nods his head, and I'm frozen in place from the intensity. "Start walking down Broom Street." He leans forward and plants a kiss on my forehead before releasing me.

His touch is gentle and unexpected. I have to blink several times before his expression changes back to the one I'm used to. The chair squeaks on the ground as I turn to do what I'm told. I'm still surviving. Just a little longer until I don't have to obey. *Until I can run.*

As I walk to the front, my legs shake and my nerves get the better of me. I turn to see the man from earlier looking at me again. As soon as my eyes meet his, he looks away from me. For some reason, my heart sinks. As if deep down I'd hoped someone would save me. How foolish.

No one in this building is coming to my rescue. I push against the heavy doors, knowing I'm the only one who can save myself.

The second the doors swing open, the cold air hits my face. They close behind me, leaving the sounds of the restaurant to fade to nothing as the noises of the night greet me. The wind lashes out at me, and I have to close my eyes and shield my cheek a moment with my arm. My thin jean jacket offers little protection against the brutal chill.

I heave in a deep breath and lower my arm. It's dark now, the sky nearly black with only a sliver of the moon shining above me. The street light closest to me flickers as I start to walk. It's only then that fear consumes me.

I'm alone. I've always felt alone, but protected in some sense. In an odd way, I've felt safe. Maybe not from my father, but safe in that I knew I'd live to see tomorrow.

The air hurts my lungs as I take in a breath, and I let out a rough cough. It makes my eyes sting as I take another step and look over my shoulder at the restaurant. I could go back, but the very thought makes me start walking faster.

Never again. My legs move of their own accord, and I shove my hands into my pockets.

I know I'll never go back. Not willingly.

If only my conviction was enough to save me. I swallow the fear rising up my throat and turn the corner. I'm bait, but I can outrun them. I'll outrun all of them. I have to try, anyway.

I blink against the wind, hating how my eyes water. I haven't cried in so long. I sure as fuck won't do it now when my freedom is so close.

Of course I'm not dressed to run. I'm in heels and a dress, with a thin set of leggings. My father wanted me to play the part of an easy target, and he had to approve of my outfit. I'm tempted to kick off the heels so I can walk faster, but that's when I sense someone behind me.

As my pace picks up, so do the steps behind me.

Someone's clearly following me.

Tracking me.

There's nothing to listen to on this empty street other than our echoing steps and my anxious breath. The smacking of his shoes against the pavement resonates loud in my ears. The click of my heels is nothing compared to the thudding from whoever the fuck is back there. It has to be a man. The sound is too damn heavy to belong to anyone under 200 pounds.

Shit. Shit. Shit.

The Romanos. No. No, I refuse to believe they'd come this close to the restaurant. It's all in my head. I can't lose my chance at freedom so quickly. Maybe it's a Rossi. The thought should give me comfort, but it does the very opposite.

I'm too nervous to look back. In the movies, when people look behind themselves, that's when they have to start running. As soon as they glance back. They run, or they die. Even though in most cases running doesn't save them anyway.

I'm not fucking stupid; if I started running, I wouldn't make it one minute before he caught me. At least right now whoever it is back there is keeping some distance. For now...

I tell myself over and over, maybe he's not following me. I still have a possibility at freedom. He's just walking to his car. Or maybe he's just walking to his house or a bar at the other end of this street. But after a few blocks, the sound of him following me is unbearable. There's not much on this street. The lone gas station is closed down, and there isn't another building for a few blocks. Everything's run down and empty. My heart rate picks up as the reality sets in. *He's here to take the bait.*

A bad man is behind me, I know that much. Maybe it's the Romanos, like my father wanted. Like he planned.

Even if he's not from the Romanos, these streets are filled with bad men late at night.

If the stranger behind me had good intentions, he would've said something by now. There's no way in hell he's not following me. At some point he'll get closer. He'll gain more speed than what I have, and then I'll have to run. But I'm definitely going to make him work for it. If he wants to put his hands on me, then he's going to have to catch me first. And then fight me. I'm not going to be a good little victim. I'll do everything possible to scratch his eyes out before I give in.

I try to steady my breath, but it's so fucking cold out, just breathing hurts.

The man shadowing me is all I can think about. I didn't even pay attention when I turned the corner down the alley.

I was so consumed by what was behind me, I didn't see who was right in front of me until it was too late.

CHAPTER 4

GIO

The Green Parrot is crowded as usual. It's a popular place in a shit neighborhood on the South Side of Chicago. We come here all the time to meet with potential clients, but usually it's just to pick up payments.

Tonight, the stakes are higher. I sit at a table with my father, a glass of whisky in my hand while he puffs away on his cigar. I take a long sip and glance at him.

"Let me do the talking," I say.

"Why?" he grunts.

"Because I'll be the one doing the job." My voice is hard, but he doesn't seem to notice.

"Doesn't matter. I'm the elder here. They came to me."

"No," I say, trying to keep my annoyance under control. "If you want to do the talking, you can do the killing."

He looks at me, eyebrows raised. "That how it is now?"

I stare back at him, but we both know I'm bluffing. My father may be a piece of shit asshole, but I owe him everything. He's still family, even if sometimes I wish he wasn't. Without him, my darkness would have consumed me a long, long time ago. But at the same time, it's because of him that it's even there.

I don't have a chance to respond because up toward the front of the bar, the doors open and grab my attention. In walks Marco Romano, the second-in-command, and second most important man in the entire *familia*, followed by Alex and Angelo, two of my cousins. They're there for muscle and show, but they aren't necessary.

Nobody would dare touch Marco. He has the full weight of the Romano *familia* behind him, and any dumb fuck that came at him would invite the wrath of the whole fucking mob down on his head. They'd go for his family and torture them all in front of him and then kill him. The Romanos don't fuck around.

The tips of my fingers trail up and down the glass as they walk into the bar.

"They sent Marco," my father says to me underneath his breath, sounding surprised.

I have to admit that I'm surprised as well. Normally we don't deal with the top members of the Romano *familia*, at least not in person. Sending Marco here to talk with us is an honor. As much as I don't want to get too involved, I do feel a surge of pride that they're showing us this respect.

But it also means that this hit is very, very important to them. I knew that when we got the target, but now it's very clear how seriously they're taking it. My eyes dip to the floor and my body heats as I realize how pissed off they're going to be when I turn them down. I can already see that my father's excited and fucking delighted that they sent someone as powerful as Marco to this deal, and he stands up to show the proper respect.

I stand also as the men approach the table, but I'm prepared to disappoint them. I don't give a fuck who asks me to do it. I'm not going to be held responsible for this shit.

"Bruno," Marco says with a smirk, "you look good, you old bastard."

"Marco." My father and Marco shake hands. I'm pretty sure that they're very distant cousins, maybe related by a distant marriage. I'm not sure. It's all so fucking boring and complicated though. They're no family to me.

"Gio," Marco says, turning to me. We shake hands. "You look just like your mother."

"Thanks," I say. I suspect the reference to my mother was designed to throw me off balance, but I keep my face and tone neutral.

"Sit, sit," my father says quickly, gesturing to the empty seats. Marco takes a seat at the head of the table, the feet of the chair scratching along the floor as he pulls it out. Alex and Angelo sit at a nearby table without another word, looking serious and tough.

I give them a little grin, but they don't look at me, and don't make eye contact. I know they're afraid of me, and have been since we were all boys. I remember when I was ten and Angelo was thirteen. He tried to take my bike, and I beat the fucking piss out of him. He's been afraid of me ever since then.

And he should be fucking afraid.

"I'm honored that you came to this meeting," my father says, practically deep throating Marco's cock. I straighten my shoulders and turn my attention to Marco.

"It's an important meeting with our best men," Marco says in return.

We are his best hitmen, that's true, but he's buttering us up pretty fucking hard. I can smell the shit he's trying to shove down our throats from a mile away, and I know where this is going.

"Let's talk business," I say before my father can steal any more momentum.

"Okay Gio," Marco says, smiling at me. He's in his fifties, and only a few years younger than my father. His teeth are straight and white, and his hair is cropped close to his scalp. He wears a dark suit complete with a crisp, white pocket square, like always, and I can see the bulge of the weapon in the holster on his side. He looks like a used car salesman wearing an expensive suit, and that's more or less accurate.

Assuming used car salesmen extort, murder, deal in prostitution, and generally engage in all manner of illegal shit.

"You're offering us triple for this job," I say, leaning toward him. "That's more than fair, given the situation."

"I thought you'd think so." His eyes sparkle and his lips turn up, as if he thinks we're eager to accept.

"Except you neglected to talk about the politics involved." He holds my gaze, but that glint in his eyes fades.

"The politics?" he asks, feigning innocence. He waves his hand in the air as if dismissing it. As if taking out a major member of the Rossi *familia* means nothing.

"If we do this job, it'll spark a war. You know this, and yet you want us to do it anyway."

"I don't know anything about a war," he says, the smile still there.

"Okay, fine. It's none of our business, I know that. We're not in the *familia*."

"Yet," Marco says, cutting in with a glance to my father.

I can practically see my father salivating at the comment.

"But it will involve us," I say before my father can speak up, feeling my irritation rise. "Regardless of the outcome."

"Do you want more money?" he asks me straight.

"It's not the money." I shake my head slightly, keeping eye contact.

"You're hesitant. I can understand that. You're young,

and don't know how the world works yet."

I clench my jaw and have to restrain myself from smashing his face into the hard maple table top. "This is a dangerous job regardless of my age."

"How about this," he says. "I'll throw in the niece of our, uh, target. You can take her and train her for us. Or at least break her down some. You know the drill. I hear she's quite a beauty."

I'm taken aback. A woman. They're giving us a woman. *What the fuck?* The *familia* has never made an offer like that before. That's not an aspect of this business I'm associated with. My father is though.

He quickly speaks up before I can even process the extent of what Marco offered.

To train? My body's stiff with the memories of my past flashing before my eyes as my father answers him. "We'd be honored, Marco," he says. "Gio will accept the woman and turn her into the perfect model of obedience for you." I've seen what they do. I know exactly what they want. I recall the sounds, the images. My father standing over a girl, a whip in his hands, a smile on his face. My heart races as I try to ignore my recollections. "You want a slave, he'll make her fucking perfect. Isn't that right, Gio?"

My father stares at me waiting for an answer, and I'm at a loss for words. I know what they mean by training, and I've seen it a million times, but I've never taken part. I've never done anything but witnessed it when I was a boy.

I'm barely able to nod my head.

"Very good," Marco says, and my father shakes his hand. "You two will do this contract, and you," Marco points at me, "will break the girl in. I'm sure your father has taught you a thing or two." Marco winks at my father, who grins proudly. "Then we'll discuss your full payment."

I blink, surprised. My father has a huge smile on his face. Before I can speak up and tell them that we won't be taking the contract, Marco stands. My father stands with him, and the two men glance at me. I stand as well, shaken and surprised at this turn of events.

"I trust that you two will come through," Marco says.

"Of course," my father responds.

"Good." Marco nods at me. "Gio, I'll send you the details so you can pick up the bonus."

Marco turns and leaves, followed by my cousins.

I grip onto the table as they leave us. "What the fuck just happened?" I hiss at my father.

"I accepted the job," he says, glaring at me. "What the fuck was that?"

"Nothing," I say, looking away. I can't admit to any weakness, especially not now. Not to anyone.

"We're doing this job," he says, his tone low and menacing. "You'll take the girl, and you'll do what you need to do. Understood?"

"We'll see," I push the words out through clenched teeth.

CHAPTER 5

GIO

If I'm going to do this, I'm doing it the right way.

That means planning. Preparation. Research. The days are long gone where a hitman could just run into a joint, shoot his gun, and run away. I need to be prepared for absolutely every and any possibility, because it's all happened to me in the past.

My father gives me shit over the planning, but he didn't have to deal with what I deal with back when he was still in his prime. Drones, DNA testing - hell, a single hair could give me away. I have to be aware of all of that, every little thing that could possibly give me away and ruin the hit.

This time it's different. This time I'm being given a new assignment, something I've never done before, but at the same time it's something I'm too familiar with.

I lean back in my chair and shake my head, trying not to let myself get lost in those memories again. I pull up my laptop and start researching the girl, Grace. It doesn't take me long before I find out most of her information.

She's beautiful, just like Marco said. She's a mob princess, so she's probably used to being treated like royalty. Except it's strange, there's not a lot of stuff about her on social media. I'd expect a mafia princess like her to have an active Instagram or something, but instead it's mostly a wasteland.

There are only a few pictures, and her Facebook profile is pretty dormant. It gives me enough to go on, and at least I know what she looks like, but it's very strange there isn't more.

I can't help but wonder about this Grace. Who is she? Who is this woman I'm going to have to break down?

I lean back and take a deep breath before standing and walking over to a window. Duke looks up at me as I walk past him. I don't pay him any attention, because he wasn't around back then. He doesn't know what it was like.

My father wasn't always in this business. Before he was a killer, he was a sex trafficker.

Maybe that's putting it too lightly. My father had a huge network of men in eastern Europe that would kidnap young attractive women and smuggle them over into the United States. From there, my father broke them utilizing a whole slew of methods, many of which he taught me over the years.

I'll never forget his favorite method, and the night he first showed me. It was late, probably after midnight, and I was already in bed. He came upstairs reeking of vodka and woke me up, then forced me to follow him. He took me out back into the old horse stable we had out there.

But of course, it wasn't a horse stable. The inside had been gutted and renovated, turning the old horse paddocks into cells with thick steel doors. Inside each cell was a woman.

I was ten years old.

He brought me into the first cell on the left where a girl maybe sixteen years old was huddled in the corner. My father told me to stay still and watch as he took his belt off and beat the girl until she obeyed him. By the time he was finished she was bleeding and crying, but at least she was down on her knees with her forehead on the ground, submitting to him.

"See, son?" he said to me. "That's how you break a girl for the first time. She needs to know that she's a rotten piece of shit, and without me, she's nothing." He spit on the ground before pulling me out of the cell, leaving the girl alone in her agony.

I hated him, but I didn't know why. His methods were cruel, brutish, and awful. But he had other methods, some clever. They played on the women's desires and fears, created a bond of friendship and trust. He only used those tactics on women that wouldn't obey him under threat of violence alone.

He gave up being a trafficker not too long after that night. His guys got pinched overseas, cutting off his supply of girls.

Then a few women got away, forcing him to move away from the area, and he never got back into the business.

But everyone knows what he did back then. It's honestly a miracle that he never got caught, and probably entirely because he got out when he did.

That's why Marco is giving me this girl, though. Marco knows what my father used to be, and he knows that my father showed me some of his methods.

He's not wrong about that. I can break this girl and turn her into a sex slave if I want. I can do all the sick, disgusting things my father used to do. I can beat her and break her physically and emotionally without a second thought.

But I don't want to. I return to my laptop and look at her pictures again, frowning slightly to myself. I don't want to make this girl bleed and beg for her life. I have no interest in that. I'm a hitman and a killer, but I'm not a rapist and a woman beater. Maybe I have a darkness inside of me that needs to be fed, but I do still have some humanity left in me.

And she's so beautiful. There's an innocence to her pictures that surprises me.

The more I look at her pictures, the more I want her. It's completely unexpected, but I want to see her, touch her, and taste her so badly.

This deal is happening whether I want it to or not. I'm sure my father would be more than happy to take the girl and to break her, even though he's older now and not as strong as he once was. I'm sure he still gets off on that shit, no matter how gross and disgusting it may be. Which means I have to keep her away from him.

I have to take her. Maybe I'm doing it for the wrong reasons, but I need to make her mine. I'm in this already, and there's no turning back.

I reach down and absently stroke Duke when he comes over and curls up at my side. I know I'm trapped, and there's no turning back. I'm going to take Grace and make her mine, no matter what.

Maybe I'm doing it to protect her. Things would be so much worse if my father took her. Or maybe I'm doing it because I'm a selfish prick, and I'm drawn to her in a way that intrigues me.

Either way, I hate myself for it, but I'm going to follow orders. I'm going to take Grace, break her, and then I'll kill her uncle.

I turn back to my laptop and begin to make my plans.

CHAPTER 6

GRACE

My eyes slowly open, and I have to work hard not to groan at the pain pounding in the back of my head. The throbbing makes me wince. The floor I'm lying on is cold. *Where am I?* It's only a second before the memory comes back to me.

I didn't have a chance. My heart sinks as I realize how easy it was for them to take me, just as my father promised they would.

I was so full of hope when the guards stayed back and let me walk through the doors of the restaurant and out into the chill of the night.

I didn't have a chance to run away. I don't think I even made it ten minutes when three large shadows surrounded me and before I could even breathe, *whack*! The blow was delivered tight to the back of my head, and I collapsed into darkness.

My jaw clenches as anger rises in me. It was so fucking easy for them.

I deserve a goddamn chance! I wanted it. I want freedom so fucking badly, and I'd do anything to get it. But I'm too weak. Raised to be weak and helpless, that's all I fucking am. Hate consumes me, mostly for my father, but also for myself.

I finally open my eyes fully, and my heart starts to hammer. My body is like ice in that it's cold, numb, and still. I know better than to let my enemy know I'm awake and conscious.

There's a cloth hood over my head, and my hot breath goes stagnant in front of my face. As I swallow, I feel slightly dizzy. I close my eyes and focus on steadying my heart. It's only then that I take in my situation.

I can still run. If I got away from my father, I can get away from anyone. *But he let you get away*, a voice hisses in the back of my head. The pulsating pain comes back, but I ignore them both. He wants me to be a good little victim. To listen and do his bidding. Fuck him. Fuck all of them. I'll survive, and I'll escape. I won't stop until I'm free. Free or dead.

I just need to be smart and wait for the perfect opportunity. Quietly I swallow, filled with equal amounts of fear and conviction. My breathing is steady but hot, filling the bag.

My shoulder is sore, and the metal cuffs holding my wrists together behind my back are cutting into the skin. It hurts so fucking bad. I realize that I'm slumped against the wall, and I feel every muscle screaming in agony.

The pain dims as soon as I hear the door open to wherever I am. My body freezes, and nothing matters anymore. I'm alert, and all I care about is finding a way out. *My freedom.* I try to keep still and pretend I'm still knocked out, but it doesn't work.

They know.

A man's rough laugh cuts through the air as he says, "She's up."

My heart pounds, but I stay motionless. In this position, my options are limited, but I'm ready to fight. I'll do whatever it takes. It sounds like there are two men in the room judging by the two sets of steps that walk on the left side of me. I hear them sink into what sounds like a sofa, and I wait. I can hardly breathe, waiting for their next move.

This could be my chance. My father is who-knows-where, and maybe these men will underestimate me.

The fear of the unknown is what restrains my actions. I'm not going to be submissive for them. I'm not going to keep my head down and wait for them to tell me what they want from me, because I don't know if that will save me from whatever their intentions are.

In this moment I hate my father more than I ever have. I hate my life.

I hate myself for being so damn pathetic and not fighting

hard enough. Death is a comforting thought, but I won't give in to that weakness. Not when there's still a chance.

Deep voices echoing Italian words that I vaguely recall from my childhood seep into my bitter thoughts. I never learned the language. My father didn't want me to. He enjoyed being able to speak without me understanding. He sends me in here to spy, and I can't even do that. *Pathetic.* The Romanos are old school, but hopefully English will be spoken more than Italian.

I know some though. I know the words slave and princess. Both continually appear in the conversation, and I know they're talking about me. The Rossi princess. Slave. I guess that's what I am now, or at least what they want me to be. I swallow thickly, hating that my initial thought is to want to be back home. Back to that prison. No! I refuse. That's just the fear talking. I don't want to go back. Anything but that.

I turn sideways and scoot away from the sound of someone approaching. But it's useless. I fall to the hard concrete floor, my head and shoulder slamming onto the cement with nothing to break my fall. I wince from the pain and then scream from the violent hold on my arms, hauling me up and against a man's body.

I struggle against him and he shakes me violently, spitting Italian words that I assume are a threat, although I don't understand.

Stupid girl, be still. Save your strength for the right moment.

The voice I hate calms me.

The thought makes my body still, and the other man laughs at my weakness.

If only they knew. With nothing to lose, I'm the strongest I've ever been.

Small shreds of light filter through the burlap bag over my head, and I realize I'm currently outside. I must be under a street lamp, because the light quickly fades and the sound of a van door sliding open fills my senses.

My heart speeds up, but I don't react yet. I listen and try to gauge what's going on. There's a third man. I can hear him now.

The one holding me tries to toss my body into the van, but I twist and kick out as hard as I can. However I've hit him, it's enough that he releases me and I fall back to the ground, nearly stumbling, but I right myself as best as I can, bound and blindfolded.

"Fuck!" he screams out as I weakly stand, balancing my body against the cold metal of the van door.

I try to run, but a fist slams into the side of my jaw. It forces me off balance, and I fall, my head slamming against the unforgiving ground. Fuck! The worst part is that I didn't see it coming. I couldn't even try to defend myself.

The pain is overwhelming. A foot swings into my ribs, and nausea threatens its way up my throat with stinging pulses of agony.

Stupid girl. You can never run from me. You can never hide from me.

My body freezes as the words of my father haunt me, momentarily crippling me.

Another kick to the gut forces a strangled cry from my throat.

A deep voice yells out, "Don't fucking touch her!" as I hear the loud crunch of a punch and the sound of someone keeling over. I'm worried about the implications of knowing they're fighting, but I don't waste a second. I can't. I need to run.

The fools didn't tie my ankles, and I take the one chance I'm given and bolt. The muscles in my legs scream with pain as I pump them, running aimlessly in front of me with my arms bound behind my back. Light and shapes whip past the bag over my head, but I have no idea where I'm going.

I don't care, I'm not wasting this moment. I can't. I can hear him chasing me, and he's right behind me, getting closer. The sounds of his ragged breathing, and his hard steps are getting louder. The world is nothing but flickering colors and madness all around me. I scream as his strong arms wrap around my waist, pulling me into his body and picking my feet off the ground.

I don't stop screaming for help and viciously kick out in every direction as I squirm in his grasp.

I gasp and instinctively try to reach up to my neck when I feel the sharp pinch of a needle.

"You're not going anywhere, princess," he says, and the

voice is soothing, although the word princess ignites anger inside of me. I fall into darkness slowly, my hands tingling and body relaxing into a hard chest as I hear him whisper into my ear, "I've got you."

CHAPTER 7

GIO

Who a stupid fucking mess.

I toss an old box of ammunition aside and drag a bench piled with crap out into the hall. The gun room in the back of my house is surprisingly large and well built, but it's gathered a ton of shit over the years. Of course my father left me to clean the thing out alone while the girl lies there on the floor, drugged and unconscious. I have stacks of old weapons, ammo, and other nice surprises stashed away in there, and it took me forever to finally get the room more or less emptied out. It's perfect for this. Fitted with a biometric scanning lock for my fingerprint, a small full bath attached and no way of escape, it's fucking perfect.

When I come back into the room, I can't help but glance at the girl on the floor. She's still right where I left her, curled on her side in the corner of the room, and still just as fucking gorgeous as she was a few minutes ago. I can't keep my eyes off her, even though I know it's fucked up to have the sort of thoughts I'm having about a woman that's drugged and unconscious.

The entire situation is fucked up though. A few days ago I wanted to turn the contract down, but my father managed to swoop in and make the decision for me. Now I'm stuck with her, Grace Rossi, and I'm supposed to somehow turn her into a model sex slave.

I have some ideas about how to pull that off, but I've never done it before. Frankly, I don't feel like fucking doing it now. My father has a past in this shit. Not me. But I'm not letting him have her. No fucking way.

All of this is a pain in the ass, especially this goddamn mafia princess. I don't need her or want her, but for better or worse I'm fucking stuck with her.

My heart hammers as I look over every curve of her body. *My princess.*

I sigh and drag a few more boxes out into the hall. Duke is snooping through them, and I push him to the side. He wags his tail and looks at me, panting and happy, completely oblivious. I ruffle his head and step back into the room, this time making an effort not to look at the girl.

Standing in the far left corner, uncovered from years

of accumulated junk, is a large cage. I stare at it, smiling to myself. It was meant for bears, and I bought it years ago at a flea market. I figured I might have to lock up some asshole that I didn't want to kill immediately or some shit like that, but I ended up just storing it away and forgetting about it.

Now, though...

The girl stirs over in the corner.

She's beautiful. Fucking gorgeous. I keep thinking that every time I see her, my memory never doing her beauty justice. I kneel down next to her and gently lift her head up, making sure she's still unconscious.

I notice the wound on her head and grind my teeth, annoyed. That fucking asshole didn't need to hit her as hard as he did, but he got what he deserved in the end. I beat the shit out of him and his partner, the sick fuck that was kicking her on the ground. She's a tiny thing in my arms, light and easily carried. I lift her up suddenly, not really thinking about it, and bring her over to the bathroom.

I gently lower her into the tub before grabbing some rubbing alcohol and bandages from the medicine cabinet. I carefully clean and dress her wounds, then quickly check her for others. I need to make sure that the sick fuck didn't break a rib or cause some kind of internal bleeding.

There's nothing there, thankfully. Or at least nothing fresh.

Her body is covered in scars. Not every inch, but there are several in places that wouldn't normally show with clothing on, white welts in jagged shapes. I take a sharp breath as I look over them, marveling for a second at the amount of pain this girl must have been put through.

Who the fuck would do this to her?

I stand, shaking my head in anger. I adjust her so that she's in a more comfortable position in the tub, my mind straying to dark places, trying to imagine what happened to her.

My princess looks like she's been through something, though I can't be sure what. Maybe abuse, maybe some kind of accident. Either way, she knows pain, and that might be a bad thing. She might be stronger than she looks. I won't intentionally cause her that kind of pain, but things happen in my line of work that can't always be controlled, no matter how much I plan.

I get back to work, removing the mirror from the bathroom and any other hardware that she might be able to use against me or herself. When I finish, the room is just a showerhead, a tub, a toilet, and a sink. Everything else got stripped out.

Back in the main room, my mind drifts back to my childhood. My father taught me how to break down and reassemble every single one of the guns I owned while blindfolded. I carefully move the remainder out of the room and arrange them out in the hall, pausing only to pat Duke on the head. My father taught me how to torture a man, both physically and psychologically. I know every mental tactic there is. I know how to break a person and to make them completely mine if I really wanted to.

He taught me to ignore pain. He taught me to complete the mission no matter what. He taught me to be strong and capable above all things, and so far I've lived my life that way.

Even if I hate the orders, once I accept a contract I have to do what I'm told.

There's a part of me that hates how much I'm enjoying this. It's sick as fuck that I love the challenge of building her a prison in a short timeframe. I know the drugs will wear off in about another two hours, maybe even less, so I have to keep moving fast. I like keeping busy and building things, but I like staring at my princess. Her scarred body only makes me want to know her more.

Those are dangerous thoughts. She needs to remain just a subject to me, not a person. I can't risk getting close to her. That's the danger with this sort of thing: sometimes you see beyond the story you're telling yourself, and the thing in front of you can turn into a person.

Once the room is clear, I stand in the middle and look around. The cage is in the back left corner, the bathroom is on the right, and the rest of the room is empty. There are two small windows, but they aren't nearly large enough for her to get through. Plus, they're unbreakable and soundproofed. She can scream, but there's nobody around for miles. I have video cameras set up in the ceiling, and I can see every inch of her enclosure, including the bathroom. The door is impervious to both blasts and tampering and will only open with my fingerprint. When I had this room built, I didn't spare any expenses. No one can get in or out without my help. It's the perfect prison for her.

I'm about to leave, when I suddenly have an idea. It comes to me like lightning. It's the perfect way to get to her, to peel back her layers and force her to show everything to me.

It's like a game, or maybe it's something like pity for what she's been through before. Either way, it's a tool.

The cage will be her safe space.

I stare at it and remember my childhood. I remember the girls and the men doing whatever they wanted to them. I remember how they cried at first, but quickly their faces became consumed with pleasure. They learned to enjoy it.

I remember how it excited me. I remember how ashamed of that I was, and still am.

I've decided. So long as she's in the cage, I won't touch her. That'll be the deal I make with her. If she stays in that bear cage, she'll be safe from me. It's a few feet wide and long, and large enough that she can stand.

But if she leaves it, then she's mine. She'll break and leave that cage with time, and I'll do whatever I want with her. *And I'll make sure she enjoys it.* If she retreats, I'll leave her alone. I'll give her food and water, and the comfort of a blanket.

My heart thuds in my chest. I glance into the bathroom and see her in the tub. She's fucking gorgeous, and I picture her crawling from the cage, begging me to come into the room and teach her a lesson.

I grin to myself. It's the perfect little game. I need to earn her trust if I'm going to make her mine, and the cage is going to be the key to that trust.

You can't just force a person to break. It doesn't really work that way. You can beat and starve them all you want, but if you never gain their trust, then it's all over. This cage will be her safety net, and I'll be the man who gives her that safety.

I can feel the darkness inside of me celebrating as excitement courses through my veins. I'm at war with myself, hating these sick little thoughts that I've been trained to embrace, and yet aroused at the prospect of playing with her.

It doesn't hurt that she's so fucking beautiful, and with a fight in her that I admire.

I walk into the bathroom and kneel down at her side. Her wounds are cleaned and bandaged, and soon the drugs will wear off. She'll wake up and she won't know where she is, but she'll be safe. I'll explain the rules of the game to her.

And then we'll play.

I reach into the tub and scoop her up, carrying her back into the main room and gently place her inside of the cage. I leave the door open, but I make sure she's completely in there. It isn't comfortable, but at least it's safe.

I give her one last look before I leave her room, shutting the door behind me.

CHAPTER 8

GRACE

My body's so sore. It hurts from where he hit me. Daddy never hit me before. I don't understand...

I was so little, so scared. Right after my birthday party. Only six. Mommy said we should leave. She took me from bed late at night and carried me into the hallway. Mommy, no. "We can't leave Daddy!" She covered my mouth and stared at the door. It was their bedroom door. Mommy and Daddy's room. We can't leave Daddy!

I didn't understand. I was scared. My heart raced in my chest. The fear in my mother's eyes is something I'll never forget. We almost made it down the stairs. Her hand over my mouth as she carried me in her arms.

But he grabbed her hair. Daddy was so quiet until he yanked her backward, the pain on her face evident as I fell from her arms, crashing onto the stairs and tumbling down. She screamed as he hit her over and over.

It hurt so much. My hands covered the gash on my head.

No, Daddy! Why is he hitting her? No, stop! I yelled with tears streaming down my face. I ran up to help her.

Daddy's hurting her! Stop, daddy! Why is he hurting Mommy? Doesn't he know he's hurting her?

He kicked me. His hard foot landing in my gut, I fell harder. Smacking my head and shoulder on the wooden stairs as I fell down another step.

It hurt, but Mommy wasn't screaming anymore.

His hands were around her throat. I didn't know it then, but he was choking her. Her fingers clawed at his hands. Her eyes turning red.

I screamed. I ignored the pain and ran faster up the stairs, hitting him as hard as I could.

Stop hurting Mommy! Daddy, stop! Please stop! My throat hurts from screaming. Someone help! Please help!

He let her go and she fell on the stairs. She wasn't moving and laid there. So still. Mommy? I just wanted to touch her. I wanted to make sure she was okay.

Her eyes were so red. "Mommy!" I cried.

His hand came down hard across my face. Mommy wasn't okay. Daddy wasn't either.

My hands covered my face where the sting from his hand pulsed. But my chest hurts too. Everything hurts. Nothing's okay.

My body's stiff as I groan, slowly opening my eyes. My head hurts. He hit me again. I feel so dizzy. The memories of my nightmare are slowly fading. Fuck, how many times am I going to let them hit me? Over and over, that's all they ever do.

It takes a moment for my sight to come into focus. And when it does, I stay as still as possible, my limbs frozen with fear.

Where the fuck am I? My heart jolts in my chest as I realize the thin silver bars I'm seeing and the grated floor beneath me form a cage.

I'm in a cage. My skin pricks with fear.

Yesterday comes back to me in a flood. My hands instinctively fly to my stomach, remembering the kicks, and then my neck, the pinch. They drugged me and put me in a cage.

My initial shock and confusion quickly turn to fury. I moved from one fucking cage to another. Only this one is a literal goddamn cage! My heart speeds with anger, and my blood rushes in my ears.

I ball my fists and turn onto my knees slowly, barely making a sound and taking in my surroundings. I'm surprised by my rage; I'm not used to it. At least not used to it showing on the surface. It's a constant, but it's generally buried under the fear and need to display obedience.

My eyes widen when I look forward and realize the door

to the cage is open.

I blink several times and even creep out slightly, but not very far at all. My hand reaches out, half expecting the door to slam shut, but it doesn't. How... odd.

As I move, a thin blanket that I was balled up in slips down my back and to my waist, exposing my chest to the cooler air. It's only then that I realize I'm naked, the breath stolen from my lungs. It looks like someone has neatly folded my clothes from earlier though, and they're sitting in a corner of the cage. I move to check my bra, and inwardly let out a sigh of relief when I see the baggie is still concealed in the padding.

I grip the blanket tighter around me, sitting on my knees. I take in a ragged breath and let a hand drift down to my sex. Did they hurt me? I don't feel any different. I don't think they touched me. Shame floods my cheeks.

I wish I'd run faster. If only I'd walked the other way. Maybe they wouldn't have been waiting. Maybe I could have gotten away. A lump grows in my throat, but I calm myself. *If*s are useless. They make me weak to dwell on them. I raise my head and focus on what's in front of me. I'm here now, and I need to figure out why and how to get the fuck out.

The grate on the floor makes my knees hurt, but I withstand the slight pain and look around the empty room. That's all it is. There isn't much I can see beyond this cage, which is large enough for me to stand, but only has a few square feet to move around in. There's a doorway, although it looks like the door has been removed, on the far side and then another door to my right.

Anxiety fills my blood.

Is this a game? Choose one door and what? I'm afraid to know.

It looks like the open doorway leads to a bathroom. It looks stripped and bare, but it's there. I imagine it's functional.

I don't dare leave the cage as I consider what the Romanos want from me. I slowly back deeper into the cage and nearly scream when my back hits a bucket. It's empty and it makes the only sound in the room other than my own voice. It scared the shit out of me. I'm quick to cover my mouth and silence the shrill scream that threatened to surface. It was only a squeak of what it would've been.

As my heart finally calms and the stupidity of my action weighs in my mind, I hear a faint beep from the door to my right and then a click.

Someone's here. Goosebumps prickle down my body as I clutch the thin blanket closer to me and back into the far corner of the cage, the farthest I can get away, kicking the empty bucket to the front. Right now my options are limited. There's not much I can do at all. But I'll bite, kick and scratch whoever's coming in here. I won't let them get away with this.

They took my chance at freedom. They better give it back.

The door slowly opens as I wait with bated breath.

I see a tray first. It's silver, and sitting on top is a small, dark blue plastic cup as well as something else. It's balanced in his massive hand as the man enters. My heartbeat slows as the door clicks shut and he turns, facing me with piercing blue eyes. They're almost like ice. His gaze freezes my heart and my rage, anger, and confusion all vanish. In their place is lust.

His corded muscles ripple as he walks toward me with confidence and an air of authority. His presence alone makes my heart stop. The way he carries himself makes it obvious that he's the epitome of power and control. It terrifies me while it also does something else. It ignites a fire in me that I didn't know existed. It's dangerous. *He's* dangerous.

His bright white shirt is pulled tight over his shoulders, and his faded jeans are hung low on his hips. So low that I catch a glimpse of the deep muscular "V" at his lower abdomen as he walks, and my lips part with a hunger to see more.

I swallow thickly as he closes the space between us. He's a Romano. Is he going to hurt me, kill me, or torture me? I'm not sure which. But whatever his plans are, maybe I can make a deal. I don't have anything he can truly want or need. I know nothing about my father's business, and I doubt they're looking to ransom me off. Taking me was a message. My father got that message, and now they can let me go.

I try to gather the courage to speak, to plead, or to fight. To do *something*. Instead my body remains paralyzed as he steps forward, setting the tray down on the floor in front of the cage.

He crouches on the floor and tilts his head, as if wondering what I'm thinking. Behind his eyes is a cold threat. His expression is completely devoid of emotion. Fear cripples me for a moment, but I gather my strength. I can't be weak. Not now.

"Wh- Who are you?" I'm ashamed of the stutter and the weak sound of my voice as it cracks. But at least I've managed to speak.

He clucks his tongue, contemplating his answer, and sits on the ground, looking into my eyes. "You can call me Gio. There's no harm in that."

My brows draw in at his comment. I don't understand. "You're a Romano?" I ask feebly. I don't think my father would lie about *who* took me, but I need to make sure.

He huffs a humorless laugh. "No, they gave you to me."

My lips part at his confession, the words slowly sinking in. *I'm a gift.* My body chills, and my throat closes and I feel as though I'm suffocating. The Rossis won't come for me. How would my father even know where I am, if the Romanos didn't take me? My breathing comes in frantic pants. No one's going to save me.

"Don't worry, Grace." My eyes dart to his. He knows my name. But I don't recognize his voice. "I won't come into your cage. You're safe there. From everything and everyone as long as you're in the cage."

He pushes the tray closer to me, and it scrapes gently across the concrete floor. It holds a cup of something, and a sandwich. The hunger in the pit of my stomach rumbles at the sight, and it makes the man smile. His teeth are a brilliant white, only adding more beauty to his gorgeous face.

It's not fair. Monsters should look like what they are.

"Eat, Grace," he gives me the command and sits at the entrance.

It pisses me off.

I'm not an object to be given away. Starting now, I don't take orders. All my life, that's all I've done. I've been told what to do, and been beaten for disobeying.

I refuse to let him do the same to me. I'm done with that. It's gotten me nowhere in this pathetic life.

"No," I barely breathe the word, knowing my defiance will earn me a beating. I don't care anymore.

He cocks a brow at me, and leaving the tray, he stands and leaves. The door closes and a moment later a beep sounds, followed by a loud click, indicating the door is locked. My heart beats faster, assuming he's coming back with something to hurt me with. I wait for a long time, staring at the door.

Time passes, and he doesn't return. I'm hesitant to think I've escaped punishment. Never has my father let a moment to beat me go wasted.

My stomach growls, and my eyes shift to the food on the tray. It's been awhile since I've eaten. I don't know what time it is, but judging from the dim light coming through the small windows, it's late. So maybe a day?

I won't eat it though. I won't give him that satisfaction.

I push more of the blanket under me and behind my back to stop the thin bars from digging into my skin and hurting.

I look straight ahead and into what's obviously a bathroom. I could leave the cage and try to find something in there to use as a weapon, but I'm terrified of leaving the safe place he gave me.

Shame consumes me. I don't even have the balls to look for a fucking weapon. My chest tightens, and I force my frozen limbs to move. I slowly crawl from the cage, my eyes on the heavy door he exited. My heart beats so hard in my chest it hurts. I don't want him to come back and beat me to the cage. *But I have to try.*

I take one step from the cage, but my fingers wrap around the bars, leashing me to it. I inhale a deep breath and let go of the bars, the thin metal slipping past my fingertips. My eyes tear away from the door and I move quickly to the tiny windows above my head.

I know it's impossible, but I have to try. I stretch on my tiptoes, trying desperately to even reach them. After a quick moment of failure, I take a step back and look at them. My body wouldn't even fit through those small rectangles. I could try dragging the cage over and climbing on top of it. I look at the rectangles again. They're so small. But I have to at least try. Even if it's just to open the window and flag someone down. Or scream for help.

I watch the door the entire time that I try my damnedest

to move the heavy cage. My shoulders ache and the bars dig into my fingers, but it's useless.

I pull with all my weight, but it doesn't even budge.

Breathless and feeling pathetic, I give up the stupid thought and my eyes focus on the bathroom. I hesitate to walk the distance of the room, but maybe there's a way out. A larger window perhaps. The windows are close enough that if I heard the click or the beep, I could easily run back to the cage and make it safely inside before he could catch me.

The bathroom is too far. I'd never manage to outrun him.

But if there's an escape, or a weapon... I only glance at the door before my instincts take over.

As quickly as I can, I dart across the room, knowing I can't fail. If he comes in now, he'd beat me to the cage. And caught in the bathroom, I'd be cornered. My heart slams with fear as I take in the barren bathroom. My bare feet slap against the cold tile as my heart pounds in my chest. My eyes dart from the steel pipe under the sink to the showerhead. Those are the only two things I can think of to even consider as a weapon. Even the toilet tank lid has been removed, and the mirror is gone, too.

I crouch under the sink and pull with all my weight on the steel pipe, but my grip slips and I fall backward, my head slamming against the tile.

"Fuck!" I shout, grabbing onto the back of my head and wincing with pain.

Click. I swear I hear a click, and I move as fast as possible. My legs scream with pain as I sprint from the bathroom to the cage. My toenail scrapes against the concrete as I nearly trip, but I keep running. I don't stop. I ignore the pain and keep my eyes on the opening to the cage. To my safety.

I slam my body against the back of the cage and breathe heavily, staring at the closed door.

All I can hear is the blood rushing into my ears and my heart beating uncontrollably with fear.

But nothing happens.

My chest heaves, and I try to calm myself as I wait with panicked breath.

Did I imagine it? I pull my legs to my chest and stare at the door.

A long time passes, and I finally realize I let the fear get the best of me.

He's not coming in here. At least not in this moment. My eyes drift back to the bathroom and the tiny windows. They're both dead ends. No weapons, no escape.

I stare at the door and wonder when he'll be back, and what he's going to do when he does return.

He said he won't come into this cage, so that's fine.

I'll just stay here, but something has to happen eventually. Something has to change. I can't be stuck here forever. The reality hits me hard all of a sudden. I *can.* This could be my life now.

In the back of my mind, I remember the bag of heroin. Hidden inside my bra. Waiting for me.

I need to find a way out of here, or else I don't have many options. Tears threaten to show themselves, and the burning pain of unshed tears is all too familiar to me.

It's been too long since I've cried. I won't cry for this man. I won't cry for me when I failed at saving myself.

There's no one for me to blame but myself.

With the dark thoughts consuming me, I fall asleep against the cage, my eyes on the food that I refuse to eat.

The days pass in a blur until I have no idea how long I've been here, and each day is the same. He comes in with a tray, taking the old one that sits at the front of my cage with untouched food. I don't even drink the water.

My mouth is dry, and my throat burns. A few times I went to the bathroom to drink from the tap, but the last few days have made me afraid to leave the cage.

During those first few days, I tested my confines. In the middle of the night, I would sneak out into the room and test everything. I went over every inch of the walls, every single corner, every single nook and freaking cranny. There was nothing.

I searched the bathroom. I ripped at the pipes, kicked at

the toilet, did everything I could. My hands are bruised and my feet bloodied from the effort, but nothing helped.

Each day was the same. He came with food and that devilish, maddening smile. He speaks so softly, so intensely. His gaze makes me shiver. I have to look away, because I keep imagining things I never thought I would.

I have nothing left. I can't escape no matter how hard I try. Days slide by, and I sneak out and do what I can, but it never helps.

Finally, the only thing I can do to keep fighting is to refuse him.

I refuse his food. I refuse his questions. I refuse everything he tries to give me. Maybe I can't break out of my prison, but that doesn't mean I have to give in to everything he says and does. I listen and sometimes I talk back, but I won't ever give him what he wants.

I think the silence and lack of interaction have done more damage than good, but I don't care. I'm so pathetic. I moved from one cage to the next. But I won't give up.

Every day I watch Gio come in and I wonder if it will be the day I leave the cage and let him do whatever he wants to me. Sometimes I even want him to break his promise and come for me. It would be better that way.

I listen to his voice as he talks to me, but I don't really hear what he says. Only the commands to eat stand out. Which I won't do. I don't care if it kills me. At this point, I'd rather die than be a toy for him. I'll just stay here and try to sleep my way to death, ignoring the pain.

During the third night, I snuck out of the cage and tried to loosen the pipes in the bathroom. It was well into the night, and normally he didn't come when there was no light left filtering through the windows. It was pitch black, and he'd never come that late.

But this time he did. I nearly broke my neck diving back into the cage as he stood in the doorway, his arms crossed, his intense stare taking me in.

Shame and guilt, oddly enough, consumed me, but fear was the leading emotion.

I'm too afraid to leave the safety of the cage now, and my body aches when I move, so it's better that I just stay still. The first two days it felt nice to walk, but now it hurts. Maybe it's because I haven't eaten, or maybe it's because of dehydration, but I'm not sure.

All I think about is the one way out that I have left. Starvation is a slow death and painful, so I should use the bag of heroin and end it quickly. But I'm a coward. And I find myself looking forward to the small bits of conversation he gives me.

There's a bed and a chair in the room now. They look comfortable, but they're tools for him. I'm not a fool. He wants me to come out so he can play with me. And I won't do it.

I wish I had more options, but the door is locked. There's no way out.

Either I submit to him, or I live in this cage, or I die.

I've held on to hope for so long. For so many years, I thought once I escaped my father I'd be free.

I escaped him only to be put in a literal cage, gifted from my family's enemies to a man with bad intentions. My pussy heats as the only thoughts that have interested me flood into my mind. I don't know exactly what he wants from me, but I'm afraid to find out. I can't help but fantasize about him using me in a way that would give me pleasure, give me a reason to live. I've only been with one man. It was a mistake, one I paid dearly for, and when my father found out, Derek paid with his life. But I'm only human, and I have urges.

I drift slightly in and out of reality, not sure whether I'm daydreaming or actually dreaming. Sometimes I'm in the cage in the dreams. It's hard to know when I'm awake, but the pain is a good reminder of what's real.

Suddenly, I move my eyes from the back wall to the bathroom and I have to blink away the confusion. Did he move the cage? My mind is fuzzy, and I look behind me and then to the bathroom. He did.

I asked him... I think I asked him to move the cage closer. Maybe a day ago, maybe more. It's so hard to remember when time runs together. But he said I had to come out. He couldn't move it with me inside. And that's not happening. I'm not leaving. I won't give him my permission to touch me.

But now, I'm closer. The cage used to be on the far wall, and now it's right next to the bathroom. I question my sanity for a moment, but I know its position has changed. I know it has.

Did he move the cage while I was asleep? With me in it? Or did he come in here? I pull the blanket tighter around me.

He said he wouldn't come in though. He promised he wouldn't. And he hasn't.

With the size of his body and all that muscle, I imagine he could've moved it with me inside. I close my eyes and see him creeping into the cage and quietly lifting me. My heart hammers in my chest, but for a different reason than I'm used to. Not fear. Desire.

My eyes snap open and I quickly run from the cage, ignoring my thoughts and go to the bathroom now that it's close enough and alleviate my needs the fastest I ever have. My muscles ache with the quick movements; it's been so long since I've stretched. There's a pain in my stomach, too. It makes me hunch over and wince, but all the while I hold my breath with my eyes on the cage. I listen, waiting for the sound of his boots outside the door and the beep of the lock. But it doesn't come. I run back and climb into the cage, and I stare at the door with my fingers curled around the thin bars. I'm waiting for it to open. But it doesn't.

Maybe he wasn't watching. I look up at the camera to my right, and then to my left. Maybe he was, and he's happy I went to the bathroom.

He tells me he'd like me to leave the cage. Maybe I

pleased him.

My head's dizzy with the thought, and my stomach hurts more than it did before, now that my bladder's empty.

Finally, my heart settles some and I move into a yoga pose, the rising sun, to stretch my aching back. The quick trip reminded me of how little I've moved; how little I've done anything.

The throbbing in my temples and the radiating pain in the pit of my stomach are constant symptoms that I'm unwell, but I can't give in. I can't live this way.

I stare at the food on the tray, but I refuse to eat it. I curl up on my side and fall into a light sleep. Only a few more days I think. A few more days until this is over.

The thought makes my heart clench, but I still ease into blackness just the same, ignoring the pain and welcoming what's to come.

It feels like only seconds have passed when the recognizable beep wakes me, and I turn slowly to face the door. Even the slow movement makes me dizzy, my mind fuzzy and weak.

Gio walks in, and his cold blue eyes are already on me.

I expect an object to be in his hand. He always brings something with him.

I'm right, there's a peach in his right hand. My mouth waters at the sight. *A peach.* The deep peach hue with a splash of gold on the side makes it look ripe. I'm sure it's sweet and juicy, and I can imagine the fuzz on my lips and tongue.

I swallow and rip my eyes away from it and stay stiff as he

walks to me and crouches in front of the cage. His classically handsome face stares back at me. It's a face that both haunts my dreams and stirs fantasies in my mind. The rough stubble along his jaw tempts my fingers to touch him. I want to feel the texture. I want to spear my fingers through his thick hair and do so much more. I close my eyes as the thoughts overwhelm me.

What's wrong with me? This isn't okay. But I can't help it. I'm consumed with thoughts of him. The seeds of sin he planted have sprouted, and I can't escape the dark thoughts.

He did tell me he wanted me, didn't he? Or did I dream it? I can't remember.

"You need to eat," he says in a low, even voice. The smooth cadence and rough tone make my nipples harden and my pussy clench. I close my eyes, ignoring my treacherous body and hating him. But I hate myself even more.

"I don't want to," I lie. I do want to eat. I don't know why I'm doing this to myself anymore. I feel weak and sick, and I hate that I let myself be degraded to this. My eyes dart to the peach in his hand, and he holds it closer to me.

"It's for you, princess." His voice is mesmerizing. *It's for me.*

A sick part of me is thrilled for a moment.

He brought it just for me. My mouth salivates as I think of the taste, and the sweet smell fills my lungs. My head's dizzy with dehydration and I don't feel well, but the sight of the peach, the gift Gio's brought me, makes me want to take it in my hands.

"Come, princess. I want you to have this." He holds it out for me, and I fall victim to the trance in his voice. I slip forward and brush the fruit with the tip of my fingers. It's barely inside the cage.

My eyes find his, and my heart slams in my chest. I'm afraid to come out any farther.

"Go on, I won't reach for you. You're safe." His words comfort me, as though I believe they're true. It's not a trick.

As I reach for the peach, his fingers gently brush along mine, stilling my beating heart and causing an intense heat to flow through my veins. The spark ignited is so intense, I nearly drop the peach, but I catch it just in time with both hands. I barely come out of the cage and look up at him, his cold blue eyes are heated and piercing into me. I slowly back away as if moving too quickly will alert him to the fact that he could touch me if he wanted to. It would break his rule if he did, but he's staring at me with a hunger that I've never seen from him. An uncontrollable hunger that elicits both fear and desire.

I push my back up against the bars of the far end of the cage and wait with the peach, my prize and gift, held firmly in both hands. My body is tense as he finally stands and leaves me in silence.

I wait to hear the click of the door and beep of the lock before bringing the fruit to my lips, practically moaning from the sweetness and licking every drop of delicious juice, wasting nothing.

It seems as though I'd only just taken a bite when I look down and see it's gone, replaced with the pit.

It wasn't enough. I need more.

CHAPTER 9

GIO

She's still in the cage. She's always in the cage.

It's impressive. Grace has gone so many days without eating, despite how weak she was when she first woke up. She was defiant, angry, and still refuses to leave the cage. She's finally accepting some food, but that defiance is still there, that beautiful fucking defiance.

In the early days, she would sneak from her cage when she thought I wasn't watching. I'm always watching her, though. I let her explore the room, test her boundaries.

I let her learn that there was no real escape.

I lean back in my chair, watching her. She barely moves, rocking side to side, humming something. I'm not sure what the music is, but she hums it sometimes when I'm not in the room. Maybe it's just nonsense and she's just passing time, or maybe it's a memory she can't help but vocalize.

I'm fascinated by her, far more interested than I thought I would be. I thought she was just another mafia princess, a spoiled little girl without a personality. I expected weakness.

Instead, I got the total opposite. According to the map of scars on her body, she's been through so much before she came to me. Because of that she has a strength inside of her that I'm not even sure she's aware of. She's resisting me far more than I ever imagined she could, and it excites me to no end.

I know that's fucked up, but I'm past worrying. The darkness is there, begging to be fed every single day. I honor my word and don't touch her when she's in the cage, which is all the time, but I ache for her to come out. I ache for the day when she finally crawls out and begs me to come into the room and touch her. I want her to beg for it so badly. I can give her a reason to continue breathing. I can make her body feel things she's probably never felt before and much, much more.

It will feel good to submit to me.

That's how I'll break her, I know. She'll finally trust me enough to call me into the room. I'll unwrap her from that blanket and bathe her, take care of her. And finally I'll slide my fingers gently along her skin and make her shiver until she pleads for more. I'll do it again and again, and soon I'll have her dripping wet on the floor, writhing with pleasure as my fingers do their work.

I'm hard as fuck just watching her on the cameras, imagining what I'd do to her. The whole thing is twisted and I feel broken inside, but I'll keep going forward. That's how I live my fucking life, just keep moving forward.

Suddenly, there's a knock at the front door. I stand up, pissed off at the interruption, and take one last glance at the monitors. She's not moving again. I leave the control room and shut the door behind me, locking it with a key. I quickly walk to the front door just as the knock comes again.

I pull it open and my father's standing there. "Son," he says.

"What are you doing here?" He never comes here. He only visits when there's a hit to be done. And that's only because he's reliant on me now.

"Come to check up on you. Gonna let me in or what?" he asks.

I nod and step aside. His heavy steps pause as he enters the hallway and looks at the mess of boxes and guns stacked in the living room.

"What's this shit?"

"It's from the gun room. I had to clean it out to make room for her."

"I know, but you didn't find a better place for it?"

"I've been busy," I say and clench my jaw and look away. "What do you need?"

"The Romanos have been asking about you." He walks

into the kitchen as if it's his and grabs a beer from the fridge. He peeks his head over the open door and asks, "Want one?"

"I'm good."

He takes a seat at the table, making himself at home and takes a big swig.

"What do they want?" I ask. I lean against the wall with my arms crossed.

"They're wondering why that bastard Toni isn't dead yet."

"I've been busy," I say again.

"I get that. But he's just one asshole."

"He's a well-guarded asshole. I've been scouting him, searching for weaknesses." I set up surveillance to learn his routines, which are minimal. He has to know it's coming. He's not giving me an easy angle.

"What about the girl? She give you anything?"

"Not yet." My blood heats at his question. She's not a part of this. I haven't asked her a damn thing, and I don't plan on it. She's not a tool to use. She's mine.

"What's taking so long?" he asks.

"You know how long it takes. They always want to rush this shit, but it takes time to plan it out." I may be putting this off a bit longer than I should. But hits take time, and they know that.

"Yeah, I get it," he grunts, drinking the beer. "Still, they're getting on my ass about it. How much longer?"

I shake my head. "Hard to say. Weeks, maybe."

"Fuck, Gio." He finishes the beer and walks back to the

fridge for another. I follow him, annoyed at this useless intrusion. I want to get back to my princess.

He knows better than this. Getting a little taste of the *familia* is fucking with his head. He knows how long it takes to research and plan a proper hit. He's complained many, many times over the years that they always want us to rush into it and get fucked, and here he is doing that same thing to me.

"Listen, I've overheard some shit," he says.

"What sort of shit?"

"There are some new meets going down. They're startng to let us in."

I raise an eyebrow. He seems excited, which is unlike him. The Bruno Luca I've known my whole life has been skeptical and quick to anger, but always patient when it comes to a kill.

I barely recognize this man. We've been growing apart for years, but now it feels like the break has finally come.

"I'm going to do it," he says, cracking another beer. I cock a brow at him and he repeats himself, "I'll do the hit."

"No," I say.

"I have a plan. You're taking too long. They want this shit done."

I ball my fists and have to take a deep breath before I clobber him to death. I almost want him to go forward with this hit and get himself killed. It would probably make my life easier if he just never fucking existed or suddenly disappeared.

Instantly I feel guilty about that thought. Although we're

growing apart, he's still my father. I disagree with him over this situation, and there are a lot of things I hate about him, but he's still my family. My *only* family. I can't turn my back on him as much as I really want to. He's given me so much in my life already.

He fucked up as much as he gave, though. Maybe more.

"I can pull this off," he says confidently.

"I'm not having this discussion." I stare at him, and there must be something in the way I'm looking at him that makes him back off.

"Alright," he mutters and takes another swig. After a second of silence, he grins at me. "Hey, let me see the girl."

"What?"

"Yeah, let me see her."

"You know I can't do that." My back straightens, and I feel a prickle of unease down my spine.

"Come on, son," he says, leering at me. "I just wanna see the girl. I just want a little taste, you know what I mean?"

"*No!*" I say, more forceful than I expected. It surprises me and clearly surprises him, because his eyebrows instantly lift up in a questioning look.

I have to scramble to cover up my reaction. "You know how this goes," I say. "I can't have you going in there and fucking up my work. I need to build trust with her, make her want me above anything else."

"Yeah," he says slowly. "Right. I know how it is."

"You can't go in there. It's not a good time." It will *never* be a good time. My heart races with anxiety, but more so anger. *She's mine.*

"Fine, fine," he says, putting the empty beer can down on the counter. "Just take care of this shit fast, Gio. The Romanos want results."

"Fine," I say, and walk him to the door. "I'll do what I can, as fast as I can."

"Alright then, son." He gives me a look that I can't read, then leaves. I shut the door behind him, breathing fast as I lock it.

As I lean against the wall, taking deep breaths to calm myself, the memory of Grace's hand touching mine comes back to me completely out of nowhere. I feel that same electric spark and excitement course through me as in that moment, and I remember her surprised but angry stare.

I didn't stop my father because I want to break her, and the realization hits me with an undeniable force.

I stopped him because I want to protect her.

I don't want my father near her because I don't want him to hurt or touch her. It's completely fucked, but I'm protective of her. The princess is mine, all mine, and I won't have anyone else come near her.

Which makes things pretty fucking difficult for me.

I go into the kitchen and make her a meal, not thinking too much about it. I'm too busy going over every detail of my conversation with my father, wondering if he got an inkling of how I was really feeling. That last look he gave me was strange.

I'm going to have to be extra careful from now on.

I carry the food on a tray to her room. I touch the fingerprint scanner with my thumb, and the door opens with a click. I push my way inside and shut the door behind me, making sure that my face is blank. She can't sense my confusion.

She's lying in the cage like always, her eyes shut, breathing slowly and deeply. I walk over and put the tray down where I always do before taking a few steps away.

"Wake up, princess," I say softly.

She stirs a little bit.

"Princess," I say louder. "Get up."

Her eyes open. Her gorgeous eyes. She looks at me for a second, then looks at her food. She shifts her weight toward me, and for a second I think she's going to come out. I want it so badly, more than I could have imagined, but instead she stops moving, those eyes boring into mine.

"I'm here for you now, princess," I say softly. "So eat up. You're going to need your strength."

I smile at her, wicked and desiring, the darkness inside of me raging with delight.

CHAPTER 10

GRACE

My lungs fill with the savory smell of cheeses and meats, along with the sweet scent of fruits.

I lick my lips, sit on my knees, and then get up on all fours, my eyes steady on the tray. This is new. I've eaten everything he's brought me since the peach, but never has he made a tray like this.

"Come out, princess," Gio says from the entrance of the cage. My eyes dart to his, and my heart beats faster. Ever since our fingers touched, there's been a heat in his eyes that I thought I was imagining. But it's there, staring back at me. I know what it means, but I can't admit it to myself. Not yet.

"I want to feed you."

I look past him at the room that used to be barren. He's brought so many things into the room over the past few days. So many tempting items to touch. Textures I haven't felt in days... I think it's been days. No, it has to be longer. I try to remember how much time has passed, but I can't.

There's a pitcher of water on a small wooden table. I imagine it's plastic, but I'm not sure because I haven't moved. I wonder if there's anything I can break and use against him, but then I look back at his intense gaze and feel a shiver down my spine. I'm terrified that the second I creep out of here, he's going to come in and take me. Never letting me go. Never giving me a chance to run back here, into the cage. I can't live here forever though, and I want to come out and see everything he's brought for me.

"Gio?" I ask, my voice surprisingly level.

The corner of his lips pull up. "Yes?"

"If I come out and you feed me," my eyes rise to his, "will you let me come back in once I've finished eating?"

His eyes narrow at me and he tilts his head, considering my words.

"Do you think I'd take your cage from you?" His voice is low, as if daring me to tell him that.

"Yes," I say, trying to keep my voice calm and level. "I'm afraid if I come out, you'll never let me back in."

His chest rises as he sucks in a breath of air and slowly releases it, never breaking my gaze. "If you come out, I'll bring you to the table, feed you, and bring you back."

My body begs me to allow it. I need his touch. I haven't felt anything other than this scratchy blanket and the cold fucking bars against my skin.

And I've thought of what the rough pad of his thumb would feel like against my skin.

"Will you touch me?" I ask him.

"You mean, will I fuck you?" A small smile curls at the edges of his lips.

"Yes," I admit.

"No, princess. I won't fuck you until you beg me." My eyes widen at his confession.

I can't live in this fucking cage forever. I crawl out, my heart beating faster and faster as I get to the opening. It's been days since I've left the cage for anything other than rushed trips to the bathroom. My muscles ache from the movement. I stop at the very edge. He's so close to me. I can feel the heat of his body.

"Gio," I whisper so softly, I can't hear my own voice over the sound of the blood rushing in my ears.

"Yes, princess?"

"Please don't hurt me." I'm ashamed of how weak I sound. I want to be stronger, but it's been so long, and I can feel myself starting to break. But something in me is telling me that if I ask him not to, he won't.

He reaches his hand out to my face, but doesn't bring it

beyond the invisible boundary. I move forward, letting him cup my cheek and pushing myself deeper into his touch. My heart swells with the gentle touch.

I need more, but I'm rooted in the cage and I don't trust him. At the realization of what I've done, I snap out of the haze that clouded my judgment. My lips part, almost as if to argue with myself, but somehow I find the strength to pull away.

I almost went to him. My heart thuds with disbelief.

I sit at the very edge of the cage, avoiding his stare. I can feel his eyes, but I don't look back at him.

My chest feels hollow and my stomach hurts. I can't live in this cage forever, but I don't want to cave to him. I feel like I've only just gotten my sanity back from the stupidity of starving myself. I have to resist him, even if I don't want to anymore. I won't let myself be weak like I was with my father.

"Sit with me, princess. I want to feed you."

I can't answer him. I can't talk to him. He confuses me and makes me question myself. I pick up the blanket and cover myself.

"Grace." His use of my name makes me look at him. There's admonishment in his tone. "You were doing so well."

The tenderness in his praise makes me question my resolve.

"I brought this in so I can feed it to you. That was the only reason."

My heart sinks. He's going to take it away.

I swallow the lump growing in my throat and shake my head.

He'll feed me something else. I know he will.

I ignore him and sit against the cage, used to the pain from the bars. He rises, leaving the tray at the entrance to the cage and stands there, staring at me, and I can't help but to look at it.

I expect him to take it, but he doesn't. Instead he says beneath his breath, "Just so you can see what you're missing, princess."

As he walks away, my fingers rise to my cheek. His warmth and touch felt... complete. I need it. I need more.

I don't want him to leave. I know this is a punishment of sorts. I refused him, so he's leaving me alone. And I hate that I want him. I want his companionship. I want him to talk to me, even though I refuse to talk back.

But I can't give in. I don't know what I'm doing; I need a plan. For now, my only defense is this cage. It's my safety but it's also a curse. I'm too scared to look beyond it. I need to though. I can't stay here forever.

I tried eating last night, and I couldn't even hold it down. I'd only taken a few bites before everything came up. I made it to the toilet, but just barely in time. I shouldn't have starved myself. I can feel my ribs, and every little movement hurts, even breathing. I need to get well. I look back at the plate of food Gio left. I need to eat.

I hear the door click open and peek up at Gio as he leaves me, the hard lines on my face softening as he turns to look at me. I watch him leave and say nothing.

CHAPTER 11

GIO

Several days pass, and I feel nothing but frustration.

Grace barely ever leaves the safety of the cage. No matter what I do to try and tempt her, she stays hidden away from me, just out of reach. She only granted me that one touch. She tempted me, teased me with that touch. She stares at me defiantly when I enter the room and looks away when I speak to her, but I see something in her glances that always surprises me. I thought I was so close. She almost came out, but in the end it made her retreat further into herself.

Nothing works. I try comfortable things, attractive things, and delicious things. The hours tick past and she ignores it all, sticking to her horribly uncomfortable cage. I know she sneaks out in the middle of the night to use the bathroom, but she runs as fast as she can and doesn't linger for longer than she has to.

I let her. I don't tell her that I know. She probably assumes as much, anyway.   There's a deep intelligence behind her uncooperative eyes that I haven't even begun to explore. I've thought about taking advantage of the situation and trying to catch her. Shutting the door to her cage and leaving her with no escape. But that's not what I want. I need her to want to come to me. But I'm getting impatient.

I can't help but question my tactics. I came into this assuming she was just another mafia princess, but my princess is clearly much more than that. She has this reserve of strength hidden deep inside of her that she's drawing from. I don't know where it comes from, not yet at least, but I want to know. I want to know everything about her.

The darkness inside of me rears its ugly head every time I go into her room, wanting to take her, use her, and destroy her. It wants to be fed, and its voice is getting louder and louder.

But there's another feeling inside of me keeping the darkness at bay.

I don't know how to explain it. It's something like a mix of curiosity and pity. I want to learn about the girl, to get inside of her head and pick its beauty clean. I also hate what the scars on her flesh mean, and I want her to give into me so that I can stop keeping her in a cage. I want her to break for her own sake as much as for mine.

But she's stubborn. Beautiful and stubborn.

I lean back in my chair, keeping one eye on the live feed of my princess in her cage while I go back through old tapes. I watch myself walk into the room with a comfortable chair and place it in the corner. I set up a table and cover it with a blanket and scarves and other warm, cozy things. She ignores it all, every single one of these items.

I stop when I get to the moment I'm waiting for. I watch as I walk into the room and get close to her cage. She moves away like she's afraid, but I pause and zoom in on her face.

It's grainy, but I can make out her expression clearly.

She's not afraid. She's *interested*. She's watching me with wide eyes, but her face doesn't betray an ounce of terror. Instead, it looks like she's watching someone she's curious about.

I skip ahead to the next day and find a similar moment. As I get close to her cage, I watch her face again in slow motion.

It's more pronounced this time. She's afraid, of course, but there's something else in her eyes.

She *wants* me.

The thought hits me like a train. My princess wants me. Her face quickly changes as I continue watching, but there's no mistaking it. I go back and watch again, smiling to myself, feeling something stir in my chest. It's a deep, deep desire for her body, a desire which I am beginning to realize she shares for mine.

I've seen that look on women's faces hundreds of times in my life. There's no mistaking it. I've had my fair share of women, and I know how they look when they see something they want. It's not always obvious, but if you know what you're looking for, it's always there.

Wide eyes. Lips parted ever so slightly. Tongue against the teeth.

My dirty little princess.

She wants to taste my cock sliding down her throat. She wants to feel my cock press between her legs as I whisper in her ear, telling her how slick her cunt is, how dirty she is for letting me have her body however I want.

I can already see it. She wants to be a filthy slut for me.

I look back at the live feed and frown again. Although she wants me, she's doing a damn good job of hiding it. She's resisting it with all of her willpower, and so far she's done an incredible job. It took me a while to even really notice it, but now I can exploit it. Use it. Break her.

Make her mine.

I feel newly energized, but my problems haven't changed. I need a new tactic, something to gain her trust.

She can't resist me forever. Hell, she doesn't want to.

I get up and walk into my main room, a plan already beginning to take shape in my mind.

I press my thumb against the scanner and the door opens. I step inside, my heart quickening the way it does every time I come near her. I slide sideways, carrying the chalkboard and the chalk in my hands.

She looks up at me, that gorgeous face almost openly curious. I walk toward her and she backs off, but I catch the look of desire. She can't hide it from me, not this time.

"Hello princess," I say, smiling. She watches me as I set up the chalkboard on top of the table facing her cage. I leave and grab a clock from outside before returning with it. I set up the clock next to the board and look back at her.

She's watching me closely. I want to walk into that cage and pull her out by her ankle and take her right here and now, but I won't. I can't do that to my princess, not until she's begging for it.

"Do you know what this is?" I ask her.

She watches me silently.

She looks thin and exhausted. I also know that she just needs to eat and sleep. The stress of the situation is making her feel ill.

"It's a chalkboard," I say. I write a time on the board: eight in the morning. I write another one down: six in the evening. I write two more times: nine in the evening, and one in the morning. She watches me the whole time, unmoving, quiet as a mouse.

"I'm changing the rules of the game, just a little bit," I say.

"On this board are a list of times. Starting at each time, you have one hour to leave the cage. I will not enter this room, and I will not touch you."

She remains silent, but I can tell she's listening intently. She moves closer to me, closer to the entrance to the cage.

"You can do whatever you want during this hour," I say. "Sleep, shower, whatever you desire. If you're good, I'll give you more time. Maybe even a few hours at night so that you can sleep." I pause and smile at her. "But only if you're good."

"How do I know you're not lying?"

Her sudden speech surprises me. I stare at her for a second, feeling like I imagined it, but no, she definitely spoke.

"Have I lied to you yet?" I ask.

"No," she says.

"No, I haven't. And I'm not lying to you now." I crouch down in front of the cage and watch her, eyes hard. "I can come into that cage any time I want, but I don't, because I made you a promise. I will keep my promises to you, princess. I'll never break them."

She stares at me, but says nothing. At least she isn't recoiling away from me like she normally does.

Emboldened, I stand up and leave the room. Out in the kitchen, I get her meal together: a delicious soup, some freshly baked bread, and a tall glass of lemonade. I carry it on a tray back into the room and place it down on the table.

She watches the food, her eyes wide. I can tell that she

wants it, and wants it badly. I've always given her food, but I'm a bastard. It's been mediocre and only there for nourishment. This is a treat. And she knows it.

"Come here, princess," I say softly. I crouch down near the cage's entrance again. "Let me hold you. Let me feed you."

"No," she says softly.

"Come," I say. "You'll be safe. I'll take care of you if you come out. I promise I'll only feed you this time." I'm hoping this time she'll give in. She'll crack, and whatever held her back before won't sneak up again this time.

She stares at me and moves closer to the entrance. Hope blooms in my chest. She's considering it. She looks me up and down with her brows drawn together. "Promise me?"

"I promise," I say. "I want to hold you and feed you. Come here." I hold out my hand.

She slides closer, close enough to touch. I reach in and gently take her hand.

My heart begins to pound in my chest. She's finally letting me touch her. I pull her toward me, being as careful as I can, but I see pain on her face. I frown, surprised.

I didn't think she was actually sick. But as I pull her out, I realize she's burning up.

She has a fever.

"How do you feel?" I ask her as I carry her in my arms to the table. I try to control my expression, but I'm worried. I didn't feel a fever two days ago. This is new.

"I'm fine," she says quietly.

I sit down with her in my lap. I can feel my cock stirring with excitement and the darkness begging to be fed, but I block it all out. I made a promise, and I'm going to keep my promises to her.

"You feel warm," I say softly. I take a spoonful of soup and bring it to her lips. She accepts it gratefully. I get another and another, and she eats every single one. *Good girl.*

"I'm fine," she says finally. I break off some bread and gently feed it to her. My fingers slip past her soft lips, and I feel the warmth of her mouth. Again my dick hardens, but I ignore it. I can feel my breathing coming in heavier, but I don't act on the thoughts screaming in my head.

I shift her weight in my lap. Her whole body rests against mine, almost like she can barely keep herself upright. She's so damn light, and I marvel all over again how easily I could break her if I wanted. She's not well, I remind myself. *I'm* not well.

It's so fucked that I keep having these thoughts. I keep thinking about taking her, breaking her, making her mine. I want to feed her and make her well again, but the darkness inside of me keeps warring against that, begging for me to go against my promises to her.

"What do you like?" I ask her, trying to distract myself.

"What do you mean?"

"For the room. What things do you like?" I need to know what the hell to get her. There's not much that I require. But nothing seems to tempt her.

She goes quiet for a second. "Music," she says.

"What kind of music?" It figures she'd ask for something that would fill the room so she can stay in that cage.

"Classical." Her voice is almost a whisper. "Piano. Quiet things."

"Okay," I say softly. "Music. What else?"

She bites her lip and looks away. "I don't know."

"That's okay," I say gently, tilting her head back to me, and feed her some more soup. Next, I hold the lemonade to her lips and she drinks it greedily. Her hands come up and hold the cup, but I control it.

"Books," she says after a few more minutes of silently eating soup.

"What kind of books?"

"I don't know. My father..." She trails off, and I can see the pain in her face.

"What about your father?"

"He didn't let me have many."

"I see." That little piece of information speaks louder than anything else has. "What else did he keep from you?"

"A lot of things..." She trails off again and I hold her close, my heart racing. I can't believe how vulnerable she is, and how much I love it. Normally I destroy vulnerable things, but right now the only thing I want to do is get her to open herself to me.

I want to drink her in.

"What did he do to you?" I ask.

"He's like you," she says suddenly. "Except also, he's the opposite." She shakes her head; confusion clear on her face.

"Did he give you these?" I ask, trailing my finger along the scars on her shoulder. She shivers under my touch and I feel my cock stir, the desire flowing through me.

She nods slowly, her lips parted, and shuts her eyes. "Yes," she says finally.

The desire leaves me in an instant. That fucking bastard. Anger boils through me, but I have to keep myself under control.

"What did he do to you?" I ask her again.

"Those were from a belt buckle I think," she says, her eyes still closed. She's practically trembling in my arms. "I was a disappointment. I'm still a disappointment. He wanted a son. But he got me instead."

"So he took that anger out on you?"

"Yes," she whispers. "For a long time. The scars are nothing. I can survive the scars."

Revulsion and hate flood through me. I realize with a jolt that I'm just like her father in a lot of ways. And I fucking hate it. I resist the urge to ball my hands into fists. He abused her for years. He controlled her, dominated her, and used her for whatever he wanted. I'm doing the same thing, although none of this was my choice.

She was forced on me. Now I'm just trying to do my job.

Lies, a dark voice whispers. *You enjoy this. You're just as sick as he is.* I don't want this. I don't want to leave scars on her beautiful body. I want to leave pleasure with my touch. It's different. I don't want to hurt her. Not like that.

"Why did you stay?" I ask her, trying to stay calm although internally I'm at war.

"I couldn't leave," she says, shaking her head. "He locked me up. He bolted my windows shut. He kept me in a cage, a nice cage, but it was a cage."

"Like this cage," I say softly.

"No," she says, and for the first time I see her smile ever so slightly. "His cage was much, much worse." Her voice softens as she adds, "He could hurt me inside of that cage."

I finish feeding her the soup and place the spoon back in the bowl. She goes silent and doesn't say anything else as I feed her the last bits of bread. I can tell that talking about her father took a lot out of her, and I'm a mess of conflicting emotions on the inside.

When we finally finish, I look her in the eyes. "You need a bath," I say softly.

She shuts her eyes tightly. "You said you'd only feed me," she points out, and there's a sadness to her voice that shreds me.

"If that's what you want, I'll put you back. But you could use a bath."

"I'm afraid."

Her confession warms me. "Don't be afraid. Let me take

care of you."

She lets out a noise that drives me fucking insane. It's a moan, or something like a moan. She doesn't open her eyes but she nods her head, giving me her permission.

I stand with her in my arms and walk to the bathroom, arousal surging through my body.

I want her. I want to take her. But I made her a promise, and I'll keep that promise.

Except her body is so soft and warm against mine, and my cock is so fucking hard. She's in desperate need for comfort, and I can give her that. I can show her what this is between us. I'm not sure I can keep myself under control. Not if she makes that sound again. I'll tear her to pieces and she'll love it, if only she'll let me.

I turn on the water, my whole body ringing with excitement.

CHAPTER 12

GRACE

The hot water fills the ceramic tub slowly. I want to hold my knees to my chest, covering myself. I've never felt more naked in front of him. Which is absurd, because I've been naked this entire time. I hardly ever have my blanket around me now. But sitting in the white tub with his eyes blatantly on my body is different.

I can't hide myself. His large hand is firmly on my thigh, his fingers just on the inside of my leg.

My pussy is so hot for his touch. It's wrong. It's so fucking wrong, but I want him to slide his hand up higher. I want him to feel how much I want him. I lay my head back and close my eyes, but not all the way. Just enough to watch.

His piercing eyes roam over my body as he cups water over my chest. The warm water feels so nice, but it runs off my breasts, leaving the chill of the air behind. My nipples harden and I watch as his pupils dilate, and he licks his lips.

Yes.

Take me. I can picture him leaning down and taking a nipple between his lips, twirling his tongue around the sensitive nub. My legs slip open slightly as the water comes up past my hips. He finally releases me, but the look in his eyes holds a warning that I better hold still.

The threat does nothing other than prepare my body for more. Arousal pools between my legs. My fingers long to touch myself. To show him that I want it.

But I don't move.

It's one thing to fantasize, but it's another to invite the danger.

And he said he wouldn't. I trust that he won't. Even as my breath comes in short pants, and he runs the soapy washcloth over my body. The gentle touch is almost too much.

My heart rate increases as the minutes pass and when he turns the water off, it's all I can hear. The thudding of my heart, and the gentle swishing and splashing of the water.

"You're so beautiful, my princess." The words spill from Gio's lips, and the unexpected compliment takes me off guard.

"Thank you," I murmur.

He cups the back of my head and gently lowers me under. He massages me and rubs away every pain.

More. I want more.

I've never had this. In all my life, no one's ever cared for me this way.

He's gentle and takes his time with me. His touch is nothing but calming... well, maybe erotic. But that's my mind playing tricks on me. Wanting me to show him how he could touch me, if only he wanted.

A voice hisses inside of me to stop this. To remember who he is. To remember who I am.

But it feels so good. When he pulls the plug and I know it's going to end, a sadness settles against my chest. The cool air is harsh, but he wraps me in a blanket and lifts me into his chest.

I'm so tired. And he feels so right. I nestle my head into the crook of his neck and fall asleep in his arms. Before exhaustion takes me over, I swear I feel his lips gently touching my forehead and hear his sweet, soft words. "Sleep, princess."

My eyes drift shut, and I already know what I'm going to see. I think of his hands on my naked body. The water felt so good. The pressure of the stream, the warmth. But his hands were a million times better. My lips part and my fingers drift over my breasts, mimicking the way his felt, but it doesn't come close.

His tender touch was unexpected, and I loved it. I wanted more. I dreamed of him taking me.

I wanted him to lay me on the bed and not in the cage. I know he promised me, but I wish he'd broken it.

I'm snapped out of my memory by the sound of Gio approaching. Rather than shrinking back from the cage, I lean forward. I glance at the clock, and the hour is up. The hour he gave me to roam freely. He kept true to his word. I thought he would, but still, I haven't left the cage since he put me in here.

My heart races in my chest knowing what I have planned. After the moment in the tub, I've been warring with myself. I want him, but I hate him. I hate myself almost as much. I've been waiting for the right time.

I have the bag, and I'm ready to use it. But not on myself. On him.

I can already see my sanity slipping. Loving his touch is a symptom that I'm not well. I'm falling into the depths of madness. I'll be shattered if I stay. I need to leave, and he has no intention of letting me go. So I have no choice. How badly I wanted him when he bathed me only proves that I'm so close to losing myself completely.

My heart lurches as the door beeps and clicks, slowly revealing Gio. I see the tray in his hand, and the cup sitting on top. And I know what I'm going to do. It makes me sick to think I can murder him.

But I need to get out. I don't know what lies beyond the door, but I know if he at least passes out, I can use his finger to get out and run for my life.

I can have freedom.

I stare into his gorgeous blue eyes and try not to show the sadness. I try to ignore the guilt weighing down on my chest. I don't know if this plan will work. But I think he'll drink from the cup if I asked him to. If I accuse him of poisoning it, and I wanted him to prove that he didn't.

I have to break eye contact as I think about how deceitful and manipulative I'm being. How wicked I am. This isn't the person I want to be, but this is what he made me.

"Will you come out for me, princess?" he asks. I nod my head, but wait at the entrance of the cage. The blanket is next to me and the bag is opened and waiting, hidden beneath it.

"Can I have a drink?" I ask him weakly. My voice cracks, and I hate that I'm showing weakness. A cold sweat breaks out along my skin. He's going to know I'm lying. My father always told me I was a shit liar. Anger courses through me at the thought of him. It's been a long time since he's been on my mind.

"Of course." Gio sets down the tray and I take the drink in my hand. It's tea. Hot tea. Perfect. I bring it to my lips and blow as Gio picks the tray back up. As soon as he rises and turns to place the tray on the table like he always does, I snatch the baggie and dump in the heroin.

I shove the empty baggie under the blanket quickly and spill a bit of the tea from the top. I gasp as the hot liquid splashes my skin and leaves a bit of a red mark.

"Careful," Gio says, quickly turning back to me. I can see

the concern in his expression, and it nearly breaks me.

"You poisoned it," I say accusingly, but I can't look him in the eye. I watch him halt in his tracks at my words.

"I haven't poisoned anything, Grace." He walks over to me slowly as I raise the cup up to him. He doesn't come closer, and I stand. I step out of the cage and hold it out to him. I keep my expression level. I can't back down now. I can't let him see through me.

"Then drink it. Please. Drink it and prove it." I look him in the eyes this time, and pray he doesn't know what I'm up to.

If I'm honest, part of me hopes he'll refuse. But he takes it from my trembling grasp and lays a soothing hand on my shoulder. His thumb rubs soothing circles against my skin.

"I didn't poison anything, my princess." With those words, he brings the ceramic mug to his lips. I watch in horror as the truth of the situation hits me full in the chest. If he drinks that tea, he's going to die. I'll have killed the only person to ever show me an ounce of respect and tenderness.

He tips it back, and I can't help myself any longer.

I reach out and whip the mug from him, scalding hot water splashing against his skin. He yells with a mix of anger and pain as the mug shatters on the ground. I stare at it, chilled to the bone. My heart pounds in my chest and then when I look up at Gio, it stills with fear.

Anger stares back at me, attempting to pin me in place.

My heart thuds once, and I bolt. He takes a large step

toward me as I reach for the cage, and my fingers grip onto the bars as he latches onto my hip.

"No!" I scream out in horror. He's going to beat me. I rip my body from him, hurling myself into the cage. Scraping my knee against the metal and bashing my forearms against the grated floor. He reaches for my ankle, still outside the cage and I look back at him, whimpering.

His chest heaves as he releases me, and I crawl to the back of the cage. I pull the blanket to me by the hem and cover myself with it as though it'll keep me safe.

He was going to hurt me. He was going to beat me.

I know he was.

For the first time in a long time, tears spill from my eyes and I can't keep them back.

I hear him pacing in front of the cage, and then he kicks a piece of the broken mug. My body jolts at the sound of it smashing into the back wall. It's not close to me, but his fury is what's frightening.

I almost killed him. I was almost free. And now I have to suffer the wrath of my captor.

I sob into the blanket and try to ignore all the warring emotions within me. The guilt and sadness, the betrayal, the anger. I don't know what to feel.

The door clicks and beeps as Gio leaves.

I've spent so many days and nights in this cage.

But I've never felt this alone and broken.

CHAPTER 13

GIO

I can't believe she did that. Anger explodes through me as I pace the living room, slowly waiting for my mind to calm itself.

She never showed any aggression toward me before. Lashing out like that was strange, extremely unlike her. I quickly go into the control room and sit down at the monitor, watching her in the cage.

I can see her trembling, practically shaking. I can't hear any noise, but I know that she's crying. I watch her carefully, the anger slowly melting away, replaced by curiosity.

Then she moves. She rolls over and looks around the room, her eyes wide. She quickly crawls out of the cage, moving as fast as she can. She grabs a large shard of the broken ceramic cup and crawls back into her cage with it. The piece is large and jagged, and I watch as she finds a hiding spot.

She goes back to her old position, not moving at all this time. I lean back in my chair and sigh, shaking my head. I know she's scared because I got mad, but she knows better than that.

What the hell is going on with her? Maybe this is a part of her process. That must be what this is. I need to be firm, and her ass is definitely going to be punished for this.

I thought we had something. Feeding her, speaking to her, bathing her... it was something I'd never experienced before. Touching her skin that way and not taking her was more erotic than anything I'd ever experienced. My blood still rings for her, and my cock's still half hard. It took every ounce of my willpower not to slide my fingers along her skin toward her tight, soaking little pussy, and part of me wishes I had.

But then there's the anger and the teacup and now this. I can't allow her to have that shard. I don't want her to harm herself. I'm not worried about her hurting me with it, because I know I can easily disarm her and overpower her if it comes to that.

But I don't want her to turn it against her own skin. She might even be able to kill herself with it. Either way, I don't want another scar on her body, at least not because of me.

There's a small problem, though. I can't just kick in her cage and steal the shard back from her. I have to coax it out of her or at least convince her to leave the cage so that I can go retrieve it. I promised that she'd be safe while she's in there, and I'm dedicated to keeping that promise.

And I'm still puzzled by what happened with the tea. Curious, I rewind the video on the monitor to my right, keeping an eye on her on the other. I return back to the moment I gave her the tea and turned away.

I have to watch it twice before I notice what she did. My breath catches in my throat when I see: she slipped something into the tea.

Holy shit.

I watch the video over and over, slowing it down, frame by frame. Sure enough, she slipped something into the tea. Something I hadn't noticed. Something she smuggled in here.

How? Why? I can't be sure. Whatever it was, she must have had it on her before she was taken. I curse myself for being so fucking careless. She could easily have killed me. Whatever she put in that tea could have been a deadly poison or a strong sedative, and if I drank from that cup, I would be dead.

Careless, fucking careless. All because I let her have that fucking bathroom. If I forced her to use the bucket, this never would have happened. She wouldn't have been able to be so fucking sneaky.

Anger rises inside of me, clean and strong. I watch the video again and again, shocked and angered that she would try and pull something like that after what happened between us.

But slowly, I begin to calm myself. She didn't make me drink the tea. In fact, she stopped me. Whatever she had in there, she decided at the last second that she didn't want to hurt me.

I lean back and take a deep breath.

This is good. Her sneaking something into the tea wasn't, but her reaction was good. It means she's beginning to feel the bond between us, that it isn't just me. She's beginning to trust me. She could have let me drink the tea, but she didn't.

I smile to myself. The shock of catching her begins to wear off, and the implications of what actually happened settle in.

Grace didn't want to hurt me. She wanted to escape, but when it came down to actually doing it, she couldn't. She stopped herself. For whatever reason, she smacked that tea cup from my hand.

She's dangerous. But that excites me more than it should.

I stand up and groan, stretching. I walk slowly toward her door, not sure if she's going to listen, but I'm hopeful. I press my thumb against the pad, making the door click open.

Once inside, I stand near the door and watch her. She's breathing slowly, not moving, and she knows I'm there. She's trying to pretend like she doesn't notice me, but I know that she does. She's shrewd and smart, a cunning little minx. I can't help but smile.

She nearly killed me. But in the end, she couldn't do it.

Now it's just a matter of time before I take her.

"Princess," I say gently. "Is there something we have to talk about?"

She looks up at me. "No," she says and looks away.

"Princess," I say, coming closer to her cage. She doesn't move. "Are you sure about that?"

"Yes," she says softly.

I sigh and crouch down in front of her. I decide not to tell her that I know what she did, afraid that it might hurt more than help. I can revisit that later, when I've earned her trust. Instead, I decide to concentrate on the shard.

"You have something," I say.

Her eye twitches toward the remains of the cup and back to me. "No," she lies.

"Princess," I say, shaking my head, disappointed. "I know you're lying."

She looks away from me. "Just leave me alone."

"I can't do that. You know I'm always watching, but you tried to lie to me anyway. Why?"

"Please," she says weakly. "Just go."

"Princess. If there's going to be trust between us, you're going to have to tell me the truth. Do you have something you shouldn't?"

She looks at me, her face stricken. I want to reach out and touch her, feel her full lips under my thumb, hear her moan as I caress her body.

"Yes," she says.

"Good girl," I say, smiling. Pride and warmth fill me. "I need you to give it to me."

"Let me keep it." Her voice is practically a whisper.

"Why? What are you going to do with it?"

"I don't know," she says.

"You don't need it. I don't want to see another scar on that perfect body."

She stares at me. "It could be for you."

I smile at her brazen response. "We both know that won't happen," I say softly. I crouch down in front of the entrance to her cage and hold out my hand. "Give it to me, princess."

She chews her bottom lip, staring at me. "What will you give me in return?" she asks.

I can't help but smirk at her. "I'll give you whatever you want," I say. "All you need to do is come out of that cage and give in to what we both know you want."

She takes a sharp breath. I know she understands what I'm saying to her.

"I-I can't," she says.

"Yes, you can. Come out, princess. Give me the shard and then let me take what I want from you."

She hesitates, but she obeys; she reaches under the blanket and slowly draws the shard out. My heart starts to rush in my chest, beating like mad. I know she's inches away from doing what we both want. I can practically already taste her delicious pussy, her smooth skin against mine. I want to sink my thick cock deep inside of her and hear her finally moan the deep release she's been dreaming about for days now.

Her hand stretches toward me, but she's still resisting.

"Come on now-" I'm interrupted by a loud knock from the other room. I can hear it clearly through the still-open door. I resist the urge to look, but Grace's eyes are drawn to the noise, her body frozen.

I pause and cock my head, waiting. She pulls back into the cage, frightened.

I hear it again, and it's loud and insistent.

"Shit," I curse under my breath. I look back at her. "Don't do anything. I'll be back."

She nods. I turn and quickly leave the room, my jaw clenching and anger coursing through my blood.

Fucking shit. I nearly had her. I was inches away, and now some fucker is interrupting us. I can't be sure I'll be able to pick back up with her where we left off. The moment is destroyed now. And I'm fucking pissed.

I head to the front door and yank it open. My father's standing there, looking annoyed.

"What?" I ask him, angry. I almost forgot about him.

He pushes past me and walks into the kitchen. "Is that how you greet me now?" he says.

"I'm busy," I say, shutting the door and following him.

He leans against a counter and takes me in. "Doing what?"

"I'm making headway with the girl."

"You haven't broken her yet?" He laughs. "Pathetic."

"She's stronger than you know," I practically growl at him. "What are you doing here?"

"The Romanos want to know when the hit will be."

"I thought you were doing that yourself."

He grunts and looks away. "Things haven't panned out."

I sigh. That's fucking typical of him. He's gotten soft in his old age and he gets too excited about bad intelligence. He probably overheard some bullshit and took it as gospel like an idiot.

I won't fall for that, though. I take my time and work things out the right way, like he used to do. Like he taught me. He's a different person now, though, a weak person. He disgusts me, and I almost pity him.

"They have to be patient," I say. "This will happen when it needs to happen. And right now I'm busy. You got me at a bad time."

He huffs, but gets the message.

"I'm making headway," he says slowly, moving back toward the front door.

"What does that mean?" I'm frustrated, and he's being vague.

"I'll be back tomorrow," he says. "There's a meeting with the Romanos. I want to talk to you before I go."

"Wait," I say. "What are you talking about?"

He pauses at the door. "You'll find out soon." He grins and leaves, shutting the door behind him.

"Shit," I curse to myself. I stand there, wondering what the fuck that's all about. I can't tell if he's just trying to taunt me, or if that little meeting had an actual purpose.

Finally, I go back into the control room and sit at the monitors. Grace is fine. She's curled up in the corner of her cage like she normally is, not moving. I think she might be asleep.

The moment is gone. I'm not sure how to recreate it at this point. I'll just have to watch her very, very closely, and make sure to stop her if she decides to use the shard. At least until I can get it from her.

I lean back in my chair, thinking about her body, my father completely forgotten.

CHAPTER 14

GRACE

It's odd. And hard to explain. I feel like I can't come out of the cage. I don't think he's angry anymore, but I still stay in here. Even during the one-hour times that he gives me to roam. Even though I crave his touch, and I look forward to him coming in, I still stay within the safety of the cage.

He came in and cleaned up the mess I made. I laid the thick shard he knew I had at the entrance of the cage and refused to look him in the eyes when he picked it up and threw it away with the others. I gave him my weapon, my only hope of escape. I simply handed it over to him. What's worse is that as he swept up the shards, I felt guilty. It was my fault that the cup was broken. I was going to hurt him. He was angry after it happened, and I thought he was going to hurt me, but he didn't. He could have come into the cage. He could have broken his promise. But he didn't.

I can't explain why it causes me so much pain.

I must be broken, I must be sick, but I prefer to stay in here, only leaving the cage for short trips to look at something or to go to the bathroom.

Gio brought in a thick blanket, and I brought it to the cage. The grate on the floor just hurt too much. I couldn't take another day of the thin bars digging into my legs. I anticipated him telling me no, but it didn't happen.

The warmth and comfort of the blanket make me want more though. I keep looking at the bed, and I want to lie on it. I want to get in the bath again and feel the comfort of the steaming hot water. I want his soothing, gentle touch on my skin.

I look to the clock. It's the only thing that makes a sound in the room, and I know I have time. He won't be back for a little while. It's my hour of freedom.

My stomach rumbles with hunger. He left the tray for dinner. He wanted to feed me, but I wasn't hungry so he left it there.

I should eat. When I eat, the pain goes away. It lulls me into a deep sleep and for a moment, I'm better. Even when I wake up, I'm okay.

But the sickness always returns in the pit of my stomach. Gio left medicine on my tray, but I didn't take it.

I must have a death wish.

I don't even know how long I've been in here. I have no plan of escape, and I don't see a way out of here.

Maybe I should give in.

I close my eyes and remember his hands on me. The feel of his hard muscles against my body.

He's offered me safety, which is something I've never had in all of my life.

I know what he wants. And I want it, too.

I don't know how much longer I can fight it. This desire to let him have me and see where this takes us. Will he make me stay here forever? I don't think he will.

I should ask him. He hasn't lied to me, and I think he'd tell me the truth. He hasn't hidden anything from me. But I've hardly asked a thing.

A small huff of a dark laugh leaves my lips and sounds crazy to my ears, but I don't care.

My father wanted me to ask questions, to listen. What a fucking idiot. The Romanos don't even have me. If he knew where I was, he'd be furious. He wasted a pawn.

My shoulders shudder slightly with a laugh, and a smile plays at my lips. It shouldn't fill my chest with warmth, but it does.

He used me, and got nothing in return. And he has no idea where I am.

The realization lifts a weight from my shoulders, and I ease into the thick blanket. He's not coming for me. That's never been true in all my life.

My eyes open and I stare blankly at the wall, the smile slipping, but what life is this that I have?

I sit up and look at the clock and the chalkboard.

I asked him for music, but he hasn't brought me any. I have nothing. The reality is that I'm wasting my time, and my life.

I don't even know what I'd do if I were to ever get out of here. I'd run, of course. But when would I stop? And where would I go?

I remember a picture my mother had in her room. It was of her family. My nana and papa. I never met them, but it was taken back when my mother was a girl. The three of them were on the beaches of France. I'd love that.

I'd love to go there. If for nothing else than to listen to the waves, and pretend I lived in their time. That I could have shared that with them.

That's where I'd run, far away. I catch sight of the chalk next to the board, and my body stirs.

I need to write it down, so I don't forget. Happiness is something that's a rarity for me, but I have it now. I can't let it go.

I look at the time, and I know I'm still safe. I don't have to run, so I don't feel any anxiety. I even stretch, letting out a yawn that creeped up on me. It feels good to move. I almost walk directly to the board, but then I remember he put clothes in the closet. They were only meant to tempt me, and so I ignored them. But now... I want to see them. I want to feel them.

There are only three simple dresses draped on plastic hangers. There's a black one with a black lace overlay. Underneath is silk. The texture feels so soft and smooth. Has it always felt this way? It's so luxurious. I eye the other two garments, which are a short red spaghetti strap nightie, and an almost identical cream one. They look beautiful, but the black one calls to me. I feel like I need it. I don't put it on though, not yet, knowing that I'm going to be playing with the chalk. I don't want to dirty the beautiful fabric.

I lay it in the cage, wondering if I'll ever wear it and quickly grab the chalkboard. It's awkward to carry because of its size, but the cage is so large, it's easy to prop up the board and sit cross-legged in front of it. I'm careful to draw around the times that Gio wrote.

I lay the piece of chalk flat and make a wave, and then another. I layer them and use my fingernail to add details to the waves. I want them to look like the ocean is drifting away.

Like they've only just come up from the current, but they're already slipping back into the abyss to blend in with the others. But in this moment, they're different.

I stare at the sketch, which somehow has texture to it although I only have the one piece of chalk. One color to work with.

I want more. I need more. I'm not able to draw it like I can picture it in my head.

I could ask him for more, but I don't want to. I don't want to have to plead with him for anything. *Other than for him to take me.*

The dark thought makes me drop the piece of chalk. My heart hammers harder in my chest.

I only know two things in this moment. Two truths which are extremely clear to me.

I need to get out of here, and that starts with getting out of this cage.

CHAPTER 15

GIO

I spend most of the day watching Grace draw.

At first I didn't know what she was doing when she moved the chalkboard. I figured she might try to write some kind of message with it and hold it up to a window, or maybe she would break it into pieces and use them for something.

But when she began to draw, I was transfixed.

I watch every movement of her body. It's beautiful the way she draws in quick, short motions, shading and sketching. I'm not surprised that she can draw so beautifully. Everything she does is impressive, and this is just one more thing that makes me believe how special she is.

Initially, I have to wonder what she's sketching. It doesn't look like much, and I think maybe it's just doodles until she begins to sketch landscapes of the outside world. I catch her staring at the walls, probably imagining what the world is like outside of her prison.

I smile to myself. Duke curls up at my feet, and I reach down to rub his head. I hope I can let her outside one day, maybe even let her play fetch with Duke on my property. I bet she'd love it out there, and I have so much land. We could ride dirt bikes or horses, or go fishing if that was something she liked. Or maybe she'd be more into picnics and wine.

I laugh to myself. I realize I'm daydreaming about taking her on a date on my property.

What a fool I'm becoming. Maybe I'm going soft for her.

I watch her draw for another hour. I'm completely happy and content just marveling at her body and her beauty when there's a knock at my front door.

That jolts me back to reality. I remember my father saying that he'd be back today, and a nervous anger lodges itself in my gut.

"Stay," I murmur to Duke before leaving the control room. I shut the door, then let my father inside. He struts into the kitchen as always, not even bothering to say hello.

The arrogant bastard is getting on my nerves.

He needs to show some respect.

I follow him. He sits down at the table this time.

"You're back," I say.

"Like I told you I would be."

He seems angry and agitated, so I'll just get right to the point. "What's going on? You mentioned some fucking meeting."

"Yeah," he grunts. "We got to give the Romanos something."

"Well, give them what you have. Since you're taking care of it."

He glares at me. "I can't get an angle, and you know it."

"You can't?" I act surprised.

"Don't push me, boy," he warns.

I clench my jaw. "Fine. What are you going to tell them?"

"Like I said, I can't get to Toni. The fucking Rossis know there's a contract on him, I don't know how."

"Tell them that. We need more time."

"I have another way."

I cock my head at him, already not liking where this is going. "What is it?"

"Toni's mother."

I stare at him for a second. "The old woman? What about her?" I ask, but I already know the answer.

"If I kill her, that'll draw that Rossi fuck out. It'll set him off balance."

I have to ball my hands into fists to keep from jamming my foot down his throat. He knows that I hate fucking with women, and especially hate killing them. Grace is bad enough, and I wish I didn't have to put her through all of this. But I can't abide another woman.

"No," I say.

"No?" He laughs. "You act like there's a better way."

"Patience," I say. "That's the best way, and you know it. This mother bullshit is just that, bullshit. You don't know what'll happen once she's dead, and that's bad. We can't plan for that."

"It's the best shot we have," he says, standing up. "Plus she's old as fuck. What's it matter?" He looks pissed, but I don't give a fuck. I want him to come at me. It'll give me an excuse to beat the piss out of him. It'll give me an excuse to hurt him for the way he fucked me up when I was a kid, leaving me with this deep darkness inside of me.

"There are lines that shouldn't be crossed," I say softly.

He grunts and finally looks down. "What about the girl?" he asks.

I shake my head. "I'm close. But not yet."

"Let me see her."

"No," I say.

"Gio." He steps closer to me, suddenly calm. "I need to give the Romanos something. Let me see the girl so that I can report back."

I stare at him for a second and finally nod sharply. "Just through the monitors, and only this once."

"Fine."

I lead him down the hallway and into the control room. Duke growls at my father, but I dismiss him with a wave of my hand. Duke slowly leaves the room, and my father glares at me.

"That dog is an asshole," he says.

"Duke just doesn't like dickheads." I nod at the monitors. "There she is."

He comes and stands next to me, and we both look in on Grace.

I can't help but smile proudly. She's in her cage, still drawing on the chalkboard, a beautiful and detailed realistic-looking shell. She looks totally absorbed and gorgeous, her face angelic and engaged in her task. I love the way she draws and how content she looks, wrapped in only her scratchy blanket.

Watching her like that, an idea strikes me. I need to get her some art supplies. Brushes, oils, canvas, all that shit. She'll love it. I smile huge. That'll bring her out of the cage. She just needs to express herself.

"What the fuck is this shit?"

I snap out of it, back to reality. My father is leaning over the monitor, squinting at Grace.

"She's in a cage," I say.

"I fucking see that. I mean the drawing."

"She's drawing," I say.

"How the fuck is that going to help break her?" he demands, standing and staring at me.

"Get out," I say softly.

He opens his mouth to argue, but he must see that I'm holding back my rage. He silently leaves the room and goes back to the kitchen.

I stand there and let the anger pass. If he had done anything but leave, I was going to beat him to death. I know it deep in my heart. I wouldn't have been able to stop. That stupid piece of shit probably thought I should be beating Grace to death, torturing my fucking princess until she did what I wanted her to do. That sick fucking freak.

Or maybe I'm the sick freak for doing what I'm doing. Maybe wanting to care for her while also making her mine is even worse.

I release a breath. No, I'm nothing like him and I never will be.

I follow him back out to the kitchen. He's leaning against the counter, his arms crossed.

"She's sick," I say.

"How?"

"I don't know."

"Don't let her die." He stares at me.

"No shit," I say. "I know that."

"We need her more than ever. We need her to be the perfect sex slave at the end of this."

The anger comes back full force, but I ignore it. "I understand."

"No, you don't." He steps toward me. "This is all falling apart. At the very least, we need to give the Romanos this mob slut as a gift if we can't get to Toni or if something goes wrong. If you can't get information from her, at least make her into a useful gift."

I grit my teeth. I don't fucking like the way he's talking. I don't like thinking about giving her back either. Now's not the time. I grunt at him, looking past him at the tray on the counter and nod. "I understand," I say, but the idea of Grace working as a sex slave for the Romanos makes my stomach turn.

There's a short silence between us. Finally, my father shakes his head and sighs. "Let's go," he says.

"What?"

"You're coming to this meeting with me."

"I thought you wanted to deal with them exclusively."

"I'm tired of being a fucking go-between, especially when you keep giving me bad news."

I watch him for a second. I don't want to go to this meeting and leave Grace alone. But I can't trust him to speak for me at this meeting. If there's something I can do to protect Grace, I need to go.

I have to trust her. I have no other choice.

"Fine," I say. "Let's go."

We follow my father to the front door. Grace is going to be okay. She doesn't want to disappoint me.

We drive in separate trucks to the meet. I don't feel like having him come back to my place after it's over, and he doesn't seem to care either way. The less I talk to him at this point, the better.

The meeting with the Romanos is at a diner at the edge of town. That doesn't surprise me, since I doubt they'd want to bring some outsiders like us into their central compound. I'm betting it annoys the fuck out of my father though. I want to sneer at him and tell him, *See? See? This is how they treat us, and you'll never be one of them.* That's useless and childish, and won't get me anywhere. He won't believe me. He'll always be looking for an in.

I need to outthink my father. I can't win this by sitting back and throwing insults at him. I know I've been too busy with Grace to concentrate fully on the hit, but I can't help myself. Now I need to figure out a way to buy myself some more time and to stop my father from going through with his awful fucking plan.

Marco rises from his seat at a corner booth and stands with his shoulders squared as we approach. The diner is full with locals and regulars, but it's really showing its age. The laminate table tops are beginning to peel, and the leather seats have holes and tears in them. The floors look like they're covered in a permanent layer of grime and grease. I suspect that this place isn't open because it does good business, but because it's just another front for the Romanos.

"Welcome," Marco says, shaking my father's hand first and then mine. "I'm glad you two are here." It's a firm handshake, but it's a mere formality.

"It's good to see you, Marco," my father says.

I nod at Marco, not wanting to debase myself by kissing his ass.

"Sit," he says. My father slides into the booth, and I sit next to him. Marco leans toward us, his hand folded in front of him, that sleazy smile on his face. "So, my favorite men. How are things?"

"Good, as always," my father replies.

Marco looks at me. "How's that little present I gave you?"

I hate that filthy smile. "She's fine," I say. My heart seems to beat slower, and my blood chills.

Marco laughs loudly. "Fine?" He shakes his head with disbelief. "That girl is more than fine, Gio. She's fucking gorgeous. You got lucky with this one."

"Yes," I grunt.

"Make any progress? I'd be interested in seeing."

I don't respond right away. I don't want him seeing. I know I have to, but I don't want to admit it.

"In fact, we were just talking about the Rossi slave. We're going to need to see how she's doing real soon." A sick smile snakes across his lips as he suggests, "Maybe a little video? Your father told us about the tapes." I turn to look at my father, that rat fuck. He should keep his goddamn mouth shut.

"We're very grateful for the opportunity," my father quickly says, that sniveling shit. "Gio here is working very hard on the girl. Right, Gio?"

"Of course," I say.

"Not too hard, I hope," Marco says. "You have a more important job to do."

This is the moment, then. I can practically feel my father ready to talk about his plan, ready to try and convince these impatient, stupid Romanos that killing some old lady would do any good for anyone.

I can't let him have this moment. "I have an idea about that," I say quickly.

My father looks at me, surprised. Marco smiles. "Go on," he says.

"Toni's well-guarded," I say slowly, the idea forming as I speak. "He's clearly the next in line for the Rossi throne, and his power is increasing every day. But what if we didn't kill him?"

Marco cocks his head at me, and my father scoffs. "Killing him is the job," my father points out.

I hold a hand up to him. "Wait. Hear me out."

"Okay," Marco says. "What are you thinking?"

"There's another man in the Rossi family that's just as important as Toni."

Recognition sparks in Marco's face. "The Don," he says.

"The Don," I agree. Visions of Grace's scarred skin flash before my eyes. *Yes, the Don.* I'm going to kill that piece of shit. I'll make it slow for her if I can.

"He's weak," my father says. "He's on the way out."

"Maybe," I say. "But he's still the Don. I think we can get to him more easily."

My father's clearly pissed. He's probably barely holding back his anger, but that's fine with me. He's the one that wanted to play these stupid fucking games.

There's no way we can really get to the Don right now though. It's possible of course, but not the way things currently stand. This is more about buying us some extra time from the Romanos to figure shit out and to plan a solid hit.

Besides, as far as I'm concerned, the Don is already dead. Maybe not today, maybe not tomorrow, but his death is coming. I'll be the one standing over him holding a smoking gun for what he did to my princess. If Marco decides to shift the target to the Don, then that'll be killing two birds with one stone, so to speak.

"Very interesting," Marco says.

"We can get to him," I say, half-lying. "He goes out with protection, but he still goes out. Toni never goes fucking anywhere. If the Don goes into the open, I can take him."

"He has guards," my father says. "That's a suicide mission."

"Not for a highly skilled sniper, it isn't," I say, staring back at him, daring him.

I can see the rage flash on his face, but he quickly gets it under control.

"Everything okay between you two?" Marco asks casually.

"Great," my father says, looking back to Marco. "Listen, I

have a different plan."

"No," Marco says, interrupting him. "That's okay. I like this. I would love to see the Don dead. Toni will have to come out of hiding to take over the Rossi *familia* duties if the Don is killed, and then we can take him, too."

"That's right," I say, encouraging his line of thought.

"Good," Marco says, nodding. "Very good. I'll take this to my Don, but I know he'll be pleased." Marco stands and slides out of the booth. I get up next, followed by my father. "Bruno, I'll be in contact soon."

Marco shakes my father's hand. "Thank you, Marco," my father says.

Marco looks at me. "And you, good job today," he says. He shakes my hand and holds it tight. "Enjoy the girl while you can. And don't take too long."

I stare back and nod, but don't say a word. I don't trust myself to speak.

Marco releases my hand. I follow my father back through the diner and out into the parking lot. My mind is full of anger at that Marco prick, but my father suddenly whirls on me.

"What the fuck was that?" he asks.

I don't stop walking. "An alternative to your awful plan," I say.

"We didn't discuss that. You didn't want to kill any of them, and now you're trying to go after their Don?" I can hear the jealousy and anger in his voice.

"That's right," I say.

"You're going to get yourself killed," my father calls after me as I walk away from him.

"I doubt it," I say softly to myself. I climb into my truck, start the engine, and pull out of the parking lot.

I'm already thinking about my princess as I hurry back home to her. *Don't take too long.* Marco's words echo in my head. I need to speed this up with her. I bang my fist on the steering wheel and curse. I hate that they have anything to do with her. But if they want to see something, I can make it happen. I have to. I can't let them take her away from me.

CHAPTER 16

GRACE

I'm debating on getting out of the cage. I've been wondering about it. Wondering what he'd do if he walked in, and I was sitting on the bed. I don't know how he'd react.

Of course, he'd probably know I was there before he even walked in. I know he watches me. But what would he do?

He seems gentle and tender, although I know that he's keeping a part of himself hidden from me. I stare at the white sheets on the bed. They're perfect and crisp. Neither of us have sat on the bed since he moved it in and put the sheets on it.

I wonder what he'd think, if I was lying there, waiting for him.

My eyes snap to the door as I hear the beep, my heart

thudding loudly. Usually I can hear him coming, but this time I didn't.

My brow furrows as he rolls in a TV cart. It's off for the moment, and encased in a large plastic box so none of the buttons can be touched.

I sit up and lean forward, my fingers wrapping around the bars.

He doesn't address me, which is odd. He always talks to me.

My heart hurts thinking I've done something wrong. I don't like that he's acting differently.

"Gio?" I call out to him without my own conscious consent.

He stops rolling the cart and angles it so it's facing the cage. Facing me. The black screen shows nothing.

"Yes?" he asks. His voice is a bit more hollow than usual. It lacks the side of him I've grown to expect. The hunger. Something's different. Something's changed, and I don't know what. But I don't like it. It makes fear rise within me.

I shake my head and shrink back into the cage. I reach for my blanket and cover myself.

Gio watches me closely, and his eyes reflect what I think is sadness.

I wanna know what's wrong. My mind is going crazy thinking of what's on that TV screen. Of what he's going to show me. It could be my father, or my uncle. Maybe it's footage of them being tortured. I have no idea, and the anxiety from not knowing fills my blood.

My instinct is to run to Gio. To ask him to hold me if it's going to hurt. It'll feel better that way. I know he can soothe the pain.

Before I can ask him anything or even move, he leaves me alone in the room. The TV is blank still and I don't understand, but he instantly comes back in with a large black plastic bag.

I sit up and wait for him to tell me what it is.

"I got you a gift, princess."

My eyes widen, darting to the bag and then back to his handsome face.

He smiles sweetly, and this is the man I'm used to. I slowly crawl to the entrance of the cage and almost slip out.

But before I can, I stop myself.

"Your drawing is beautiful." I look back to the chalkboard taking up so much room in here. I thought he might be mad. The idea that he might take it away from me also crossed my mind. So I kept it in here.

"You like it?" I ask him softly.

He walks to the cage and crouches in front of me, nodding his head. "I do," he says and his words warm my chest. "I got you more supplies. Whatever you need, princess."

My heart swells. I try to contain the emotion, knowing that something is wrong with me for even feeling remotely happy with Gio and his praise, but I ignore it and hold onto the sweet feelings.

He holds his hand out and waits. Knowing what he wants, I lean forward and let him cup my chin in his hand. He runs the rough pad of his thumb over my lips.

My heart beats faster. *Kiss me.*

I wait for his touch, but he doesn't move. I scoot closer to him, but still, he doesn't reward me.

"You'll have to beg me, princess, remember that."

My eyes widen and for a moment, I'm shocked. He's denying me? He has yet to do that, and for some reason it pisses me off.

I scoot back into the cage and resist the urge to pout like a petulant child. What the fuck is wrong with me?

Before I have time to think on it, he lets out a rough chuckle and clicks on the TV before leaving me alone again.

Sounds fill the room, and they're loud. So fucking loud. It's been a long time since I've heard music. I squint at the screen, not because the images are small, but because I just don't understand.

I don't recognize the people, and it's obviously a show.

It takes me a moment to understand what I'm seeing, but when I do, my hands ball into fists and anger consumes me. I stare at the door, willing him to come back.

It's fucking porn.

CHAPTER 17

GIO

I can't help but smile to myself as excitement courses through my veins. I watch her staring at the television through my monitors, and her face is perfect. She's enraptured, angry, confused, and clearly aroused by what she's seeing.

The idea came to me as I was driving back from the meet with the Romanos. I needed something to speed the process along, but so far everything I've tried has either been interrupted and ruined, or failed entirely. I needed something to force her to confront her feelings for me.

I needed something to get her soaking fucking wet to the point where she simply couldn't resist any longer.

It came together pretty fast after that. I got an old TV,

covered it in a plastic casing, soldered the power button down, wired a car battery to it, and streamed as much dirty fucking porn as I possibly could. I removed the volume buttons and the input buttons, so there was no way for her to turn it off or change it. She's stuck watching whatever I want her to watch.

Her eyes are wide as she watches the video. Playing on the screen, a half-naked slut in a schoolgirl outfit goes down on a thick cock. It's dirty, nasty, and the girl moans as she deep throats the guy's cock.

I'm half hard myself, imagining exactly how my princess would suck me off. Her lips are full and gorgeous, and I could see the horny slut deep inside of her begging to be let out. I know she'd take my thick cock down her throat, choke on it, gag and moan, but she'd keep working. I know my princess will work hard for me once she finally gives in.

She suddenly crawls toward the cage's entrance. She glances at the clock, and I can practically see her thought process. *You have an hour, princess,* I think to myself, smiling.

She quickly leaves the cage. I watch as she goes up to the television and begins to try and turn it off. She works the power button and tries the volume, the channels, the inputs, but nothing works. I grin, proud of myself for rigging this television. The porn continues to play.

She hits the TV out of frustration and then winces from the pain, shaking out her hand and looking at the television like it's her enemy. A rough laugh rises up my throat. She's pissed. I'm happy that she finally came out of her cage and is doing something other than sulking. Apparently, all she needed was a little hardcore porn to push her over the edge.

I lean back and watch her for a few minutes. She continues looking at the TV, trying to figure out a way to turn it off. I can tell she's considering just breaking it, but she hesitates. She's probably wondering what I would do if she broke it.

I'd just clean up the mess and bolt one to the wall. And up high enough so she couldn't reach it. I smile to myself. *Don't do it, princess. It'll only get harder for you.*

I can see the frustration on her face, but also something else. I glance at my own private feed of the porn she's watching. The girl in the uniform is getting her pussy reamed from behind. She shakes her ass, bucking her hips back against the guy, her face a mask of ecstasy. I look back at Grace and watch her reaction.

She's staring at the television. I can't really read her expression though. She's not upset or revolted by it, but she's clearly fascinated and can't look away. Slowly, she bites her bottom lip, and a smile comes to my face.

She's dripping wet right now. I can practically smell it from my room. She looks away, but I know she's thinking about how good it would feel if she let me give her the pleasure she truly craves. She's practically shaking, trembling for my touch. *Beg me, princess.* I know she will. She's going to be in need.

I stand, my cock hard, and quickly walk away from the monitors. I can't go in there yet and I know that if I keep watching, I won't be able to control myself. It's already taking everything I have to stay out of that room. I want to go in there, grab her hips, turn her, and press her against the wall. She won't put up a fight as I pin her arms behind her back and fuck her tight, slick pussy from behind. Fuck, I can feel a bead of precum leaking from my slit. I've been dreaming of taking her. This better fucking work.

I walk into my kitchen and lean up against the counter, taking deep breaths. I clear my mind of any image of her. Duke comes into the room and I pet his head for a second, until finally the desire passes.

I open my eyes again and release a breath. That's better. I have to keep myself under control. She has a little time to herself.

I go to the table and check her medicine. She's been taking it, and I can tell that she's already feeling better. I can't be sure why she got sick in the first place, and I have to wonder if it was because of something I gave her. I hate the thought that I made her sick. I sure as fuck hope she doesn't think that.

I've tried to give her what she needs. She's a prisoner, but she's treated better than any prisoner could hope for. She has her own bathroom and tub, and can clean herself during her private hours. She has plenty of food, and sometimes she has delicious food. She has things to keep her mind occupied if she decides to leave her cage.

I shake my head, trying not to linger on this. I might have caused her illness, but I'm fixing it. I'm making it right.

I pat Duke again, then head down into my basement. The wooden boards creak under my feet, and I pull the light switch at the bottom of the stairs. The room is half finished, and there's another bank of video monitors against one wall, though smaller than the one upstairs in the control room. This is my secondary monitoring station, and it's dedicated solely to Grace's uncle.

I scroll through the feeds, skipping through the videos until I get to something interesting. Toni is surprisingly strict in his daily regimen and he never, ever gives me an opening. If he's ever out in the open, it happens late at night or at a random time during the day, and it never lasts for more than a few minutes. He's a very careful man, and I have to admit that I'm impressed.

But it makes it very, very difficult. Now that my princess is becoming mine, I need to move my plan forward. It's unlikely that I'll ever actually kill the Don, and so I need to find a weakness in Toni soon. I need to exploit that weakness and murder him.

Time passes as I watch the videos, one after the other. Nothing important appears as always. Duke curls up at my feet.

When I finally check the time, I'm startled. It's been at least two hours, which means that Grace has been alone in her room for much longer than I intended. I quickly finish up and leave the monitors to continue recording before heading upstairs, Duke at my heels.

"Stay out here," I mumble to him as I go in to check on Grace. I shut the door and pull up the video feeds.

She's lying down in her cage, staring out at the television. I glance at my feed of the porn, and it's a video of a woman riding a guy, working her hips over and over. I look back at Grace and zoom in on her.

I suck in a sharp breath when I get a closer look at her face. Her lips are parted with pleasure, her breaths coming in sharp and short. I pan down and realize that her hand is between her legs working in furious motions.

I zoom out and stare. My princess is touching herself while watching the porn. She finally couldn't take it anymore. Her legs are spread wide, and I stare at her pussy as her fingers slide in and out of herself, her head thrown back, loud moans escaping from between her lips. She's baring herself to me. She knows I'm watching.

My cock is hard as fuck, and I'm pissed. She isn't allowed to get herself off without me, no fucking way. I stand, shaking my head. There's absolutely no way I was going to let her touch herself, not without me at least. If she's going to get any pleasure, it's going to be because I say she can have it.

The dirty fucking girl. I bet she's thinking about me right now, her two fingers sliding in and out of her tight, slick cunt. I'm angry that she's daring to touch herself without me, but

I'm also so fucking turned on. My cock is rock hard, straining against my jeans.

There's only one thing for me to do.

I head toward her door, intent on making her give me what I want.

CHAPTER 18

GRACE

I've never been this horny in my entire life. I'm not an innocent. I've watched porn before. Videos just like the ones playing on the screen.

I felt perverted then. Ashamed, even. My fingers trail up and down my sides, hardening my nipples. I gently brush over them. The tingling sensation is directly attached to my throbbing clit. My head leans back against the cage.

I've been listening to moans for hours. To the slapping sounds of a man thrusting his hips against a woman's ass filling my ears. I can't tune it out. I can't unsee.

At this point, I can't even look away.

My pussy pulses with need.

I can't help myself. My head thrashes as my fingers circle my clit. I need it. I need the release. I whimper as my body heats. I need more.

I can't even breathe right. I move from my position, lying on my back and let my legs fall open, exposing myself. My inner thighs are wet from my own arousal. My breasts are perky, and I grip one with my left hand for the added sensation, squeezing roughly for a slight hint of pain. I need it.

I pinch my nipple as the woman on the screen reaches her climax. I need that, too. Please. I pull back and love the sharp sting from my own touch. My legs tremble, and I'm close. So close. My back arches, but before I can fall blissfully over the edge, I hear the faint beep and the door slams open.

My movements stop, and the heightened pleasure that overwhelms every inch of my skin dims. I almost want to cry at the loss.

The sight of Gio makes it worth it though.

He looks pissed, and I don't hold back the smile that shows on my lips. His chest rises and falls as his eyes move between my glistening pussy and my face.

I circle my clit once and moan from the sweet build of pleasure.

"Grace," he says in a low voice, making his way over to me in slow, deliberate steps. "You know better than to touch yourself."

I almost laugh at him. If he thought I'd beg him, he thought wrong. I'll stay in this fucking cage and get myself off until I'm limp and numb. Unable to move and soaked from my own cum.

I circle my clit again and the sharp sensation shoots through my legs, stiffening them and making my neck arch.

"Grace!" he yells, and the rough tone of his voice only makes me want to tease him more. To piss him off. To make him punish me.

A harsh moan is ripped from my throat at the very thought of him doing just that.

Pulling me out of the cage by my ankles and fucking me, filling me with his thick cock. *Yes!* Ruthlessly pounding into me without any mercy as I scream his name.

My legs try to close as the sensation becomes overwhelming and I whimper, shutting my eyes.

"Be a good girl for me, princess." Gio's voice is soft and full of lust.

"No," I say easily, staring into his piercing blue gaze. His eyes widen at my defiance, and I love it. I love that I can shock him and use this tactic against him.

I'll regret this later; I know I will. Faintly I'm aware of the edge of my sanity screaming at me. A part of me is furious, hating myself and him. *But it feels so good.* And I've wanted this for so long. No, I've wanted more. I've wanted him.

He crouches down low, and I meet his gaze as he stares at my body. "You're going to be in trouble if you don't stop."

His low threat brings me closer to my release, and I

quicken my strokes against my clit. *Yes!* I stare at him, willing him to tell me how he'll punish me. I need him to send me over the edge. I'm so close.

I look him in the eyes and sink my fingers as deep as I can into my needy pussy. His eyes flash to my sex, and his breathing quickens. I slowly pump my fingers, curling them to stroke the bundle of nerves at my front wall and push my palm against my clit.

The sound of his belt buckle clinking as he struggles with his zipper makes me moan.

He's always shown so much control, but in this moment, he's undone. And I did this to him. My neck arches, and I have to tilt my head to keep my eyes on him as he unleashes his thick cock. My legs instinctively open wider and I rub my clit faster as he strokes his dick, his eyes darting from my pussy to my face.

"Come here, princess," he barely breathes, his chest heaving in air as his large hand moves up and down his massive length. I moan, thinking of how he'd feel inside me. How he'd stretch my walls. Would he even fit?

He'd force his way in.

The thought makes my back arch, and I strum my clit faster.

He leans forward, his free hand gripping the edge of the cage. The noise makes my body jolt, but I don't stop. He groans; anger and lust are clearly evident on his expression.

I love watching him. The sight is enough to push me

close, but then he moans my name and it's my undoing.

My body writhes and my legs tremble and finally I explode, every nerve ending igniting at once. The sensation is almost too much for me to take, but now that I've fallen, I can't stop myself.

We cum together. Thick streams of his cum splash on my thigh, marking me, claiming me as his. The action only heightens the waves of pleasure rolling through my body. I try to keep my eyes on his, but my body tightens with a heated paralyzing pleasure that I can't control, and I throw my head back.

I try to breathe, but it gets caught in my lungs. Finally, I scream his name, loving the sweet tingling sensation ricocheting through my body.

My limbs sag against the blanket and he groans, forcing the last of his orgasm out. My eyes are heavy, but I look down and see the evidence.

My middle finger slides along my thigh and wipes up some of his cum.

I can't help the smile on my face as I slip my finger into my mouth and suck. My eyes are locked with his.

He tastes sweeter than I thought he would, with just a hint of saltiness. I fucking love it. So good. I wipe more of his cum off of my thigh and savor it. I feel smug that his plan backfired, and I'm still safe in my cage.

"When you finally come out of there," he says, and the anger comes back into his voice as he tucks his dick back into his jeans. It's still partially hard and I find my legs clenching with the sweet sensation of desire shooting through me as he continues, "You're getting punished for this, princess."

It takes a moment to register what he's saying. Instead of fearing the implications, I'm curious. I want to know. Is he going to spank me? Fuck me rough? My eyes roll back in my head and I relax on the blanket, wondering what he's going to do to me.

I hear the door close, and the soft beep... and then the moans of the television. I weakly turn my head and then let anger rise inside of me, groaning with frustration.

He left the fucking TV on.

CHAPTER 19

GIO

My blood rings with desire for her as I collapse into one of my kitchen chairs. I can't think or concentrate on anything, and I'm not even sure how I ended up in the kitchen.

I can't get the image of her cumming out of my mind. Her perfect body, her full lips, her moans fill me with such intense desire. Though I didn't touch her, it was still the sexiest thing I'd ever been involved with.

The tension between us was incredible. As I stroked my cock and she watched, fucking her own pussy, I knew that she was mine. I can still feel the post-orgasm bliss as I sit here, slowly coming back to myself.

Grace is a dirty fucking girl, and now I'm sure of it. She's a fucking freak, and I'm going to bring the slut out of her. That was a good start, but there's so much more work to be done.

I'm going to make her my fuck slave. Once she gets a taste of my thick cock buried deep inside that greedy little pussy, she'll know she's mine. There won't be any other way. Once I make her back arch, her muscles clench, and her nipples hard, she'll be begging for more and more and more.

And I'll give it to her. I'll be good to her. *I'll give her everything.*

I finally get my shit together and stand. I glance at the clock and begin to prepare her dinner. I decide to make her something special, so I drink some whisky as I cook.

Duke comes into the room and watches me, head cocked, tail wagging.

"We're close, boy," I say to him, tossing him some scraps. He catches them, tail wagging. "She's driving me insane. That dirty fucking girl. She pretends to be all broken and innocent, but now I know better. Now I know what she's really like."

I go back to cooking, shaking my head. Listen to me, talking to my fucking dog. I must be really losing it over this girl. Duke eventually leaves the kitchen, heading back to lounge on his bed while I put the final touches on her meal.

A beautifully seared steak sits on top of buttery, garlicky mashed potatoes. French-style green beans sit to the side; French-style basically just means they were cooked in a shitload of butter. The delicious smell rises up to me, and I know she won't be able to resist this.

It's been two hours since I was last in there, and my cock is already stirring at the thought of going into her room. Watching her touch herself--that was just the start.

I'm going to get more, and soon.

The door clicks open, and I step into her room. I glance around at the space, smiling to myself at all of the luxuries I've provided her with. My gaze ends up on Grace hiding in her cage, the porn still playing in the background.

"Hello, princess," I say to her.

"Are you here to punish me?" she asks with a slight smile. She's breathing heavy and lying on her back in the cage. I can't tell if she's mocking me or not. It gets me hard either way.

"Not yet," I say, and place the tray down on the table. I know she can smell the delicious food.

I stand in front of the entrance to her cage. She stares back at me, not moving. The blanket covers most of her body, leaving her shoulders and her legs exposed. I stare at her skin and remember how she looks with her fingers pressed deep inside of her pussy. I know she's soaking wet and tight, and I know she's yearning for it as much as I am.

She's gorgeous, so fucking gorgeous, and she needs to be fucked. She needs my thick cock to teach her what she really wants.

"You look hungry," I say to her.

She glances at the empty table with her forehead pinched in confusion, then looks back to me. "No. I'm okay."

"I'm not talking about food." I kneel down in front of the entrance to her cage.

She watches me, curious. "What do you think I'm hungry for?" Her voice is breathless, and her eyes clouded in lust.

"I think your body is hungry for my touch," I say. "You sit inside that cage day in and day out imagining what I'd do to you if you finally came out, don't you?"

"No," she says, but she doesn't look away. Her blanket slides down ever so slightly, revealing the tops of her breasts.

"You're thinking about it right now. What would happen if you let me touch you?"

"Nothing good," she whispers.

"No," I say, smirking at her. "It won't be good at all. It will be very, very bad, princess. And right now, your body craves bad. Doesn't it?"

"I don't know," she admits in a small whimper, and that sends a thrill through me.

"I know," I say staring at her intensely. "You're aching for it. Right now you want to throw off that blanket and crawl over here. Go ahead, princess. Crawl over to me."

She watches me silently for a second, then obeys. She slowly gets on all fours. The blanket drapes loosely over her back, but I can see her perfect breasts, the incredible line of her flank down to her beautiful hips, and I'm hard as a fucking rock.

"What will you do if I come over there?" she asks.

"I'm going to give you what you want. We both know I can, princess. We both know I can make you feel things you've only dreamed about. You don't have to be in a prison with me. Submit, give in, and I'll make you feel free."

She stares at me, biting her bottom lip, and crawls toward me. I stay still, watching her. She stops near the entrance to the cage. I could easily reach out and touch her, but that would break my promise. She's still behind the entrance, and safe.

"What happens if I do that?" she asks.

"You know it won't hurt," I say in a low voice. "And if it does, you know you'll want that hurt. You want it because it'll make the pleasure that much sweeter. Let me make you feel it."

"How?" she asks.

My heart begins to hammer hard in my chest. This is the moment I've been waiting for.

"Turn around," I command.

She hesitates, and I wonder if she'll obey. I'm left dangling there for a moment, hanging on her every move, until she slowly turns around.

"Lift the blanket up," I order.

She does it. She lifts the blanket up over her hips, revealing her perfect ass and her slick, dripping pussy. Fuck, she's so gorgeous. I unbutton my jeans and slide my hard cock from my briefs, slowly stroking it.

"Come closer."

She takes a sharp breath. "I'm afraid," she admits.

"Don't be. You know you can trust me. Let me make you feel good, princess." My voice is husky and low with desire.

She slowly backs toward me. Slowly, agonizingly slowly, she lets her ass cross over the threshold, but then she stops.

I can barely hear over the pounding in my chest. I reach out and softly caress her round little ass. I want to slap it and make her moan, but not yet. I need to start with pleasure before I give her pain. I slide my fingers down her skin until I feel her tight, wet pussy.

Fucking hell, she's so turned on. I hold back a groan and the need to slam my dick deep into her cunt. She's absolutely soaked. "You dirty girl," I whisper as I slowly slide my thick fingers inside of her. She groans, looking over her shoulder and lowering her upper body to the floor of the cage. "You're dripping for me. You can't deny it anymore, princess. You want me."

"I don't know," she moans. "I don't know what I want."

"I do." I press my fingers deep inside of her tight little cunt, marveling at its slickness. She's so fucking pretty, pink and perfect.

"Fuck," she groans. "More."

"Don't tease me, princess. Come closer."

She inches closer. I grab her hip with my other hand as I tease her pussy with my fingers, sliding in and out, moving up to tease her clit before finger fucking her again.

Grace tips her head back, her moans getting deeper, more insistent. I can read her body as her pussy gets wetter, and her moans get louder. I know what she wants. I know what she needs.

"Gio," she groans. "Oh God, Gio. That feels so good."

"You never really knew how good I can make you feel, did you? Now you know. Now you're going to beg me for more, aren't you?"

"Yes," she gasps as I press my fingers deep inside of her, curling them to find her G-spot, sliding in and out. The sounds fuel me to give her more. "Oh God, yes."

"What do you want, princess? Say it."

"I want more," she moans. "I want so much more."

"You greedy fucking girl." I grin, loving this. My cock is practically twitching, yearning to get inside of her. It's almost time. "Is that what I've made you? Just a greedy slut?"

"No," she moans. "I'm not greedy."

"But you are a slut for me. We both know that now."

"Yes, fuck," she moans. "I'm whatever you want, Gio."

"That's right. That's what I want to hear." I slide my fingers out of her, making her whine and glare at me. "Come closer," I say.

She slides a bit farther out of the cage. Half of her is outside. I spread her legs wide and gently caress her soaked pussy with the tip of my cock, teasing her, loving the way it makes her squirm.

"Gio, please," she says, and so I press myself deep inside of her.

"Oh shit," she gasps, tossing her head back. Her arms stretch out in front of her, and her fingers claw at the blanket.

"Fuck," I grunt. Her pussy grips me like a fucking vise as I press myself deep inside of her. I slide into her so easily. Her pussy is aching for me, so fucking wet for me.

"Gio," she moans as I slide back out and in, fucking her slowly at first.

"That's right," I say. "Take this fucking cock. This is what you're meant to do."

"Yes," she moans. I grab her hips and fuck her deeper, a little bit faster. I reach around her hip and find her clit, carefully teasing her sensitive spot.

"Oh God," she moans, her voice louder and lower, losing control. She tries to buck me off, trying to get away, but pushes herself back onto my cock not a second later, her legs trembling with need.

"That's right," I say, moving slightly back. She follows me, slowly moving out of the cage. "You're my dirty princess now. Ride back against this fucking cock, girl. Don't be a greedy slut."

She moans and starts to work her hips in time with mine. She bucks back, sliding back and back, riding hard against my cock. I grunt, pleasure threatening to overwhelm my mind.

I grab her hip with my left hand and spank her ass with my right. She groans, but it only makes her work harder and faster. I can tell she loves it. I know she's starting to realize that a little pain makes the pleasure sweeter. I slap her again and again, leaving light red handprints on her ass, but it only spurs her on. *Smack!* The sound fills the room, making my breathing come in short pants.

She rides back against me harder, her whole body shaking, her hair spilling down over her shoulders. We're moving backward as our pace increases, rutting and fucking there at the entrance to the cage.

Soon, only her head is still inside of the cage. I reach forward and tease her breasts, pinching her nipples as I rail into her. Pounding that sweet little pussy of hers and giving her every reason to love what I'm doing to her. We inch back, fucking deeper and harder, until finally, finally, she's completely out of the cage.

That sends me into a fucking frenzy.

"Fuck, Gio," she practically screams. "Yes, Gio, fuck me. Fuck me. Make me feel more." I give her what she wants, slamming into her, losing myself in the rough fucking.

I reach forward and grab her throat and pull her back against me. She gasps as she realizes where we are in the room.

"You're mine now, princess," I say into her ear, my cock buried inside of her.

She moans and writhes against me as I pick her up, one hand on her throat, my cock still buried deep inside of her, and carry her to the bed.

CHAPTER 20

GRACE

My pussy is still spasming on his thick cock as my hands dig at his fingers, trying to pry them away. Fear, bliss, and lust are all mixed within me and make my heart race.

He's not holding my throat too tight. It's just instinct making me try to push his hand away. He lifts me from the cage, and my heart beats faster as I weakly struggle against him.

I'm practically impaled on his dick with one of his arms braced against my front and between my breasts, his hand squeezing my throat, and his other hand gripping my hip.

I struggle to breathe as waves of a dim release threaten to consume me. *It's coming.* I try to writhe against him, both to get away but also to feel more. I need more.

He lays me on the bed and spreads my legs so he's straddling one thigh, his hand still firm on my throat and he squeezes tighter.

For a moment, only a fraction of a moment, my heart freezes with fear, a distant memory breaking through the pleasure. My mother. Her death. His fingers dig into my throat and I kick as hard as I can, uselessly. This is different. I try to separate the two, I try not to be afraid. But I am. I'm so fucking terrified.

Small white circles dance in my vision as he pounds into my pussy, thrusting deeper and harder, relentlessly taking from me. The moment of fear and conscious recollection passes, and waves of pleasure consume me.

My mouth opens with a silent scream as I cum violently. His grip on my throat loosens and he lets go as the ecstasy rocks through my body. He rides through my orgasm, viciously fucking me and making the intensity of my release that much higher. I feel lost in bliss, unable to do anything but claw at the sheets.

He thrusts into me without mercy as I scream with pleasure. Wanting more, but trying desperately to get away. My body is propped up, and I'm trying to just hold on. And then his fingers strum my throbbing clit, and I can't take any more. My lungs still, my body goes stiff and every nerve ending explodes with a fire I've never felt before.

He groans my name and his thick cock pulses inside of

me, his hot cum filling me and leaking between us. It's only then that I can breathe, with his lips barely touching my neck as he pumps short shallow strokes, prolonging his release and sending shivers down my body.

He presses his lips to my neck and I breathe easy, a feeling of longing overwhelming me as I hold him closer. But as quickly as it came, it's gone. He pulls out and moves off the bed, leaving the chill of the room to creep closer to me. I watch his back as he walks to the bathroom, and the reality of what's happened slams against my chest.

My breathing comes in frantic pants, and my eyes go wide. I'm not safe. I don't waste a moment. I don't listen to what he's doing; I don't even try looking for him. I climb off the bed and run to the cage, not stopping until I'm in the very back corner and covered by my blanket. His cum leaks down my leg, and my heart squeezes in my chest.

What have I done? What's wrong with me?

I don't know what's worse, the fact that I enjoyed what happened or that I didn't even realize what I'd done until he left me.

He holds a spell over me, his very presence a trance. I can't escape it. He's like a drug, and I've grown addicted.

I watch as he walks back into the room, stopping only two steps from the bathroom. His brow furrows as he looks from the bed to the cage.

And then his eyes flash with something else. Something

I've truly never seen from him.

Anger.

He looks fucking pissed. His hands ball into white-knuckled fists. His eyes narrow as he locks onto my gaze, forcing me to maintain eye contact and he stomps over to the cage.

I try to scoot back farther, away from him and his rage, but I can't. I'm cornered.

But I'm safe.

My heart beats faster.

He won't come in here. I'm safe here.

But I'm not.

He doesn't hesitate to bend down, walk straight into the cage and grab me by my ankle. He yanks me toward him, and I yell.

My fingers try to grip onto the bars, but they slip as he pulls me into his chest.

I scream and try to kick away.

No! He lied! He lied to me! My heart tries to climb out of my throat as fear consumes me.

"Stop fighting me, princess," he says quietly and his voice is gravelly low.

My blood runs cold, and I still in his arms from fear of what he's going to do. I knew it was too good to be true. I'm not safe. I never was.

He brings me to the bed, and I wait for his fury to be unleashed. My body sinks into the mattress, and I keep my eyes closed.

But nothing happens. I pull the blanket tighter around me, as if it can protect me. It never has before, but I have nothing else. There's nothing left.

After a moment passes with the only sound being his heavy breathing, I open my eyes.

The bed dips and groans as he sits on the bed, his back to me.

I don't understand.

"You won't ever do that again." Gio's voice is hard, unforgiving. And I cower behind him. "Do you understand? I'll take your cage away if you dare leave me like that." He finally turns to face me, and I can see the hurt in his eyes. "You will let me give you aftercare, do you understand that?"

My heart's racing, and I feel so confused. He leans down and kisses me. His tender touch is so unexpected. My heart swells, and tears leak down my cheek.

I don't understand it.

He pulls away with his eyes still closed and says, "You don't leave me after something like that. Not until I say you can." He opens his eyes. "You need to be comforted. Do you understand?"

"Yes," I answer weakly.

His eyes roam over my face, searching for something. "Are you okay?" His voice is so soft, so calm. It's a side of him I haven't seen.

I nod my head, but my fingers slowly rise to my throat.

An asymmetric grin pulls his lips up. "Did you like that?" he asks, his fingers touching mine and then sliding down my throat.

I can't lie. I didn't. I shake my head slightly, and concern is written all over his expression.

"Please don't," I shut my eyes and I can't continue.

"Shh," he leans forward and kisses my jaw and then down my neck and collarbone.

"I thought you enjoyed it... You didn't..." He clears his throat and looks away. "You didn't want any of it?" he asks.

"No!" I'm quick to correct him. "Just the choking."

He looks back to me and considers my words. I can tell he wants to ask.

"I watched my dad kill my mother," I say softly. I hold his gaze as it softens.

"My princess," he whispers, lying next to me and pulling me into his hard body. It's not until my cheek is against his bare chest that I realize I'm crying. I never cry. "Never again, I promise you."

"And I won't leave you." I say the words so quickly, and for a moment I misunderstand myself. Or maybe I meant it to be literal, I don't know.

He holds me until I've stopped crying and then kisses my hair, whispering, "I need to clean you up." He leaves my side and turns back to give me a look of warning. But I don't want to run. I want to stay. I don't want to hide from him.

I feel vulnerable and raw, and the way he holds me makes it seem as though that's just right. It's the way it's supposed to be.

When he walks back into the room, he seems different. I'm not sure why, but everything now is so different.

My thighs tremble slightly as he slides the warm cloth between my legs. I'm still on edge from hours of stimulation. He gentles his hand on my thigh and moves me to lay on the bed on my side. I curl up as he lays the blanket on top of me, tucking me in and moving behind me, his chest to my back.

He feels so warm, so strong. And his smell is so comforting. I fill my lungs with his masculine scent. It relaxes me. The tiredness of the day settles against me, lulling me to sleep in his strong embrace.

"I was supposed to punish you, princess," he murmurs and kisses my neck.

"Next time you touch yourself without my permission, you'll be punished. Is that understood?" His voice is hard, but he's holding me with such tenderness that the threat falls flat. Besides, I don't want to touch myself without him. I want him to take me like that again and again.

I want more.

"Yes." He holds me closer, and my heart beats frantically.

I'm vaguely aware that this is wrong and that I need to use this new development to my advantage, but the voice is so weak, drowned out by the steady beat of his heart, that it's easy to ignore. If only just for this moment.

CHAPTER 21

GIO

I pour myself a double whisky on the rocks and collapse into my couch in the living room. Duke comes over and curls up at my feet. I scratch his head as I sip the whisky, staring at the blank TV, my mind wandering over what just happened.

I've needed a strong drink since the second I first saw her. I needed to feel her tight pussy, to hear her scream my name, to know that I was making her feel intense and unbridled pleasure. Finally, I got what I needed, and my blood's practically ringing with incredible contentment. But I got more than I bargained for.

I regret going into her cage. I wish I hadn't done that. I promised her it would be her safe space, and I worked so hard to keep it that way. I just couldn't allow her to go back into her shell, not before I properly took care of her. She needed to be caressed, cleaned, worshipped. She needed to be shown how I feel about her.

Maybe I shouldn't have gone into the cage. I could see the fear in her eyes, and I hated that. But afterward, it was worth it. She let me take care of her, stroke her hair, whisper in her ear. Finally, when she was relaxed, I left her dozing on the bed.

She's dangerous; she makes me want to take her to my bed. To let her out. To share more with her. And that can't happen.

She's so fucking gorgeous. I can still feel her tight cunt wrapped around my cock. I can't get enough of her lips, her skin, her moans. It's all so fucking intoxicating. I know I have another job to do, but the idea of going out and killing again when I have my princess to train seems insane to me.

Now I'm faced with a new issue. I need to start that training, but I'm not exactly sure how to go about it. I've never actually turned someone into a sex slave before, and I still don't want to do that to Grace. She's my princess, not my slave, and I want to be the only one to have her.

I clutch my glass, the ice clinking against it as I feel my darkness rising up again. Lately it's been so quiet, probably because I was so content with Grace. But now that I'm faced with the prospect of killing her father and turning her into a slave, I can feel that darkness rising.

I want to make her mine. I want to dominate her. And I

want to slit her father's throat for every bit of pain he's shown her. He fucking deserves it. The darkness wants all that, too, but for a different reason. The darkness in me wants it because it wants to destroy everything in its path. I want those things because I care deeply for Grace, much more deeply than I ever imagined.

My two halves are still warring, but I know which one is winning. I know my humanity is still there, and it feels stronger every day. There are moments, just like this one, where my darkness rears its revolting head, but I can get past it.

I will get past it. For Grace. *For my princess.*

I take a long sip and scratch behind Duke's ear. He looks up at me, head cocked, mouth slightly open.

"You want Grace to stay, don't you boy?" I ask him.

He pants a bit. I smile at him.

"Of course you do."

I stand up and knock back the rest of my whisky. As I head into the kitchen to get some more, I hear my phone buzzing back on the couch.

Annoyed, I head back and grab it. I don't recognize the number, but it's a local area code. I decide to answer it, though I don't usually take calls from strangers.

"Hello?" I say into the phone.

"Gio." I cock my head to one side. I vaguely recognize the voice.

"Who's this?" I ask.

"Where do you live?"

I narrow my eyes. "Who is this?" I ask again in a hardened voice.

"Where are you staying? Do you think it would be hard to cut off your fingers?"

My blood runs cold. The more he talks, the more I'm sure I know the voice.

"Listen, asshole," I say softly. "I wouldn't threaten me if I were you."

"We know all about it. What time's it going down, do you think? We're always watching you, Gio."

"Alessandro," I say. "That's you, isn't it?"

The voice pauses. "Soon, Gio. We're coming for you soon."

"Listen to me, you Rossi fuck--"

But he hangs up before I can finish.

I stare at my phone, not sure what the fuck to make of that conversation. My heart's pounding against my ribcage, and my anger starts taking over.

I can't be sure, but I thought the person was Alessandro, one of the Rossi cousins. I met him a couple times and he was just another one of their low-level scumbags, not someone I would ever worry about.

But that call is disconcerting. The mention of my fingerprints makes me think that he knows about my door, and my heart clenches at the thought. She's mine. No one else has a reason to go near her.

They didn't protect her from her father.

They can't have her back. I won't allow it.

I pace the living room, analyzing every second of the phone call. I need to be smart. I need to stay one step ahead.

I stop in my tracks, realizing they must know about the hit. Which means there's a rat. A rat with a big fucking mouth, ready to start a war. I have no clue how that's possible, since nobody that knows about it has any reason to tell the Rossis. The fact remains that the call happened, and it did not bode well.

I toss my phone aside and walk into the kitchen. I fill up my whisky again and as I head back into the living room, an uncomfortable thought strikes me.

Was my father so far gone that he would sell me out to the Rossis?

I stand completely still as my mind races through the possibilities. I know that the Rossis would love to have me, even before all this shit with Grace and killing Toni and their Don happened. I've killed Rossis before, and I'd probably do it again.

But no, no, that couldn't be it. My father wouldn't do that. He's an old man in a business that's not kind to old men and he's desperate to be relevant again, but he's not a fucking traitor. He's family. *We're* family. And that's an impossibility. Besides, he wants to be a part of the Romano *familia* so badly. Making a deal and selling me to the Rossis would destroy his chances at joining the Romanos. Even he would have to see that.

I'm just being paranoid. I walk over to the couch and sit

back down again. This time, I flip on the TV and stare blankly at the football game, not really paying attention. Duke sits by my feet as I sip my drink, my mind roaming over the possibilities.

I can't shake my suspicion. I want to, but I can't help it. I keep imagining my father making a deal and selling me out, no matter how implausible.

"Fuck," I say and stand up. I finish my drink and feel the alcohol loosen my nerves. "I'm being stupid," I say to myself and walk into the kitchen. I put my glass in the sink then head into my control room to check on Grace.

I have to put the call out of my mind. It was meant to get to me. I need to be better than that. Better than this.

I can't worry about it just now. My father wouldn't betray me. I know he's close on a plan to finish the Don once and for all. He's come through countless times, and I know he'll come through now. I saw parts of the plan, and from what I can tell, it's solid. I wouldn't go with him on the hit if it didn't look like a serious plan.

The call was probably just some bullshit prank that the Rossis decided to test me with. I have to concentrate on Grace now that we're doing so well.

I sit at the monitors and watch her, slowly forgetting about everything else.

CHAPTER 22

GRACE

I don't know why I came to the cage. But now that I'm here, I can't leave. I slept so well on the bed. It was a deep sleep, full of comfort. But he was gone when I woke up. The sheets beside me were cold to the touch. And it left me feeling like I'd been cheated. I don't know what's wrong with me to think there's more to what this is.

Yesterday ruined me. It destroyed my armor. I don't recognize the woman I am.

I've sat here all day, feeling hurt and abandoned. As if I have a right to feel those things. What did I expect? I'm nothing to him. I'm no one. A piece of property that he was gifted.

My jaw clenches and I refuse to feel any more for him,

but the second I hear the thudding of his boots in the hall, I take notice. My body turns to the door, and I wait for him. I'm eager for him. I hate it, but I won't lie to myself. As much I detest this side of me, I find comfort there. I even *enjoy* it.

At least I'm in the cage. My lips threaten to curl into a smirk, but I resist. If he wants to leave me, then I can leave him, too.

The door beeps, one of my favorite sounds now, and Gio takes two steps into the room. I watch his eyes as they move from the bed to the cage. Anger isn't present, not like it was last night, but there's something there. Or rather, something's missing. That spark and fire, the heat in his eyes. Something's different, and it throws me off balance.

"Grace," he greets me, walking to the large chair by the table. He sets the tray in his hands down and looks back at me, sagging into the seat. He leans back and waits.

I want to crawl to him. I want to put my head in his lap and comfort him.

I know something is wrong. I just don't know what.

My heart stills as I wait. Both of us are staring at each other, but neither of us are willing to act.

Finally, he moves forward, resting his elbows on his knees and resting his chin in his hand. "Come to me," he says softly. My body obeys before I give my conscious consent. I move forward on all fours.

I crawl to him, partly because I want to and partly because I know this is one step closer to my freedom.

Yes. I cling to that reason. I convince myself that if I'm a good girl, he'll let me go. I've gotten good at lying to myself over the years.

I'm not obeying because I want to submit to him, I want to please him. That's not why.

I'm not hurting for him because something's wrong. I don't feel for him. That's not what this pain in my chest is.

I can tell myself lies all day and night, but the moment I reach him, kneeling on the concrete before him, and he leans down, cupping my cheek in his hand and pressing his lips to mine, my heart swells.

I arch my back and moan into his mouth, my fingers spearing into his hair and pulling him closer to me.

Gio.

He breaks our kiss and sits back in his seat, his eyes never leaving mine. I stay kneeling on the floor, eyes wide and waiting for him. For whatever he wants from me.

"Do you think you can obey me?" he asks.

My eyes narrow, and for a moment I don't respond. But I swallow my hesitation and nod my consent. He won't hurt me. I trust him.

He rises and walks over to my cage. He looks back at me as he grabs the door that's been pressed against the side of the cage this entire time and swings it shut. Closing my cage, with me on the outside. The loud clicking sound ricochets in my head with disbelief.

My heart pounds with anxiety. I back away slowly on my ass until my back hits the wall.

Fear threatens to creep up on me, but Gio doesn't move.

He raises his hands in the air, and talks in low tones, as if he's approaching a wounded animal. And maybe that's just what I am.

"It's alright, princess. I just need you to know there will be consequences."

I feel like I can't breathe.

"You said you wouldn't take it away." I can barely get the words out. They're forced.

"I won't," he says softly, "it's just one hour." Instinctively, I turn toward the clock. One hour.

"Do you trust me, princess?" he asks.

My chest rises and falls with heavy breaths.

It takes a moment, but I can admit it. I do. I trust him.

"Yes," I whisper in a shaky voice.

"Come here." I start to stand, but he adds, "I want you to crawl."

I debate on whether or not I want to. Not because there are consequences, but because I don't want to obey. At least for that moment I don't, but I remember the look in his eyes when he came in here, and I move to him. I crawl, wondering if this will ease whatever troubles he has.

I want to ask him. But I don't know if he'll answer. As I sit on the floor next to him he reaches down and moves my legs so that I'm kneeling. He backs away, appraising me. It pisses me off.

"When you come to me, you'll sit like this." I look down at my body, and then back up to him. The cage is to my left, and it's closed. I bite my tongue. If it were open, it would be a different story. For a moment I consider how he'd punish me. What he'd do.

Would it be worth it to disobey?

"Now lie back and grab your knees so I can see you." He walks a few feet away and turns to face me, arms crossed, waiting for me to obey.

Yeah, it's fucking worth it.

"No." My voice is strong, and Gio immediately reaches for me. His hand is out like he's going to grab my throat and I shrink back, fear crippling the strength I have.

But he doesn't grab my throat at all. He picks me up by the waist and quickly walks to the bed, throwing me over his lap.

I don't even have time to react as he throws one of his legs over mine and immediately slaps a hand down on my ass. *Smack!*

My back arches as I scream out from the blistering pain, but he holds my shoulders down, forcing my upper body into the bed and continues the blows.

Again and again he spanks me. Each time in a slightly different spot, and they burn with pain. It radiates from my ass outward. Fuck, it hurts! My brows pinch, and I try to get away. But I can't.

Finally, it's over, but the cold air only makes it hurt worse. I try to move away, but he keeps me still.

Gio massages my sore ass and says in a low voice, "Stop running from it."

I wince from the pain and wriggle away, but he only holds me tighter.

"You want this," he says, moving his hand to my pussy. He shoves his thick fingers inside of me without hesitation and my body bucks in response, but he pumps them in and out, stroking my front wall and sending a heated bolt of desire through my body.

He pulls them away before I can climb toward my release, leaving me wanting. I'm surprised at how wet I am and how easily he pressed his fingers inside of me.

Bastard!

"Suck," he says, putting his fingers in front of my face. I could do it, and a part of me wants to. I want to get lost in this moment. My breathing comes in frantic. *I just need to obey.*

"Do it, princess. Don't overthink this." He leans down, whispering in my ear. "What we have is perfect. Enjoy this with me."

His words are my undoing. Just the acknowledgment that something is here between us makes me shed the last of my inhibitions. I take his fingers into my mouth and lick them clean, tasting my arousal. I moan while sucking on his fingers.

"Good girl," he says, kneading my ass. I wince from the sudden pain, and he chuckles.

"Now," he moves from the bed, leaving me alone on top of the sheets. "Get on your back and pull your knees up."

My heart slows, and I swallow my pride.

Is it wrong to give in when I want it? I shift on the bed, and a hint of pain from the spanking makes me suck in a sharp breath.

"On your back, princess." He waits while I make my decision and finally lie on my back for him.

I grab under my knees and lift them so he can see all of me. I watch his eyes heat, and it erases any trace of shame I have. He *wants* me.

I hide my smirk as he falls to his knees by the bed, so he's eye level with my pussy. He takes a languid lick and I moan, leaning slightly to the left.

His hand comes down hard on my inner thigh with a loud *smack*!

My body jolts and I quickly move away from him, but he drags me back to the same spot, holding me down.

"Don't move," he warns me. His eyes pierce into mine, daring me to talk back, daring me to move, but I obey.

Partly because of the shock.

He waits until I'm in the same position and then runs his finger down my pussy and up to my throbbing clit, circling it once. The pleasure makes me want to move, but I stay still.

"You're so perfect, princess," he says moving away from me and leaving me on edge. He takes a step back and looks me over appraisingly. My cheeks heat, and I feel a small sense of anxiety now that the heated look is gone from his eyes.

"Kneel," he says and I quickly move and sit in the position he wants. His large hand wraps around my thigh and moves my legs slightly apart.

"Like this." His hard voice forces my eyes to his. "Remember that." I hold his gaze and nod once.

"I want to train you," he says softly. "Would you like that?"

I speak before I can think, "Yes." y eyes widen at my confession.

"Good," he says with a small smile, and the look he had when he first came in shows itself again as he sits on the bed next to me.

I start to move, but then stop myself. I need to be still.

He chuckles and places his large hand on my thigh. "Training is over for today, princess." There's a sadness in his voice, and I don't like it. "Tomorrow we'll start again. Not today."

I slowly move, not understanding Gio's motivation. Something's changed between us, but more than that, something's wrong. I know it in the core of my very being.

"Are you alright?" I ask him. I can't help it. I don't like that something's bothering him.

He tilts his head and considers my words before nodding once. "Everything will be fine."

"What's wrong?" The only thing I gathered from that response is that something is not fine. And I want to know what.

He runs a hand down his face and then pulls me into his lap. I love the feel of being this close to him. I find myself melting into him. The comfort is something I've never had before, and I don't want to lose it.

"I'm supposed to do something that I don't want to do," he finally says.

"Don't do it then," I say simply.

He outright laughs at my response, leaning against the wall and pinching the bridge of his nose. "If only it was that easy, my princess."

I lean against him and listen to the steady sound of his heart.

The memory of everything that's happened flashes in front of me as I stare at the cage on the other side of the room. I look at the clock, and the hour is up.

I don't want to tell him though. I'm not ready to go back. *But I don't have to, do I?*

I frown, realizing my initial thought was that I should be in there. *In a cage.* I shouldn't be. I shouldn't even be in this fucking room.

I look up at Gio and wonder what he's thinking. I wonder what his plans are for me, but I can't ask. All the time I've been here, I've never asked. I know I'm a gift. I know he wants me.

Maybe this thing between us is real. Maybe he feels what I feel. I'll never know if I don't ask. But my blood runs cold.

What if it's not the same for him? What if I'm mistaken?

"Gio," I gather the courage to ask, my breathing quickening with the fear of what his answer will be. "I don't want to stay in this room anymore." I can't look at him as I ask. But the lack of an immediate answer makes my eyes rise to his piercing blue gaze.

He watches me for a moment, and my heart clenches. Something's wrong with me to think that he'd care what I want. But I did. I thought... I don't know what I was thinking. Just before I move to pull away from him and search for the woman I used to be, he pulls me closer into his chest.

"This won't be forever, princess." He whispers his words. I don't resist, but there are so many unanswered questions, so much more that I need to know.

"If I'm good--" I start to ask, but he presses a finger to my lips, silencing me.

"You're perfect. And I promise," his eyes pierce so far into me, I'm mesmerized by his gaze. "Soon, everything will be different. I promise you."

His words are vague, but I trust him. I lean into his touch and press my lips against his. This is all I need right now.

Emotions overwhelm me, my body heating with a mix of anxiety and something more, something that's sinful and dangerous. Something vulnerable and raw.

Gio breaks our kiss, and I feel lightheaded and breathless.

"Come sit on your throne, princess," he groans, lifting me

as though I weigh nothing and spreading my thighs apart as he lies on the bed and lowers my pussy onto his face.

His tongue laps at my sex as I grip onto his hair and nearly collapse forward from the sudden intense pleasure.

He doesn't let up. Licking and sucking and making my body shudder in utter pleasure, he's relentless.

I throw my head back and moan his name, "Gio."

He groans into my pussy and sucks at my clit, forcing a scream from my throat. *Yes!* I grind my cunt into his face, wanting more and being so close, so soon.

"Cum for me, princess," he whispers, lifting me off of him before spearing his tongue into my opening.

All form of common sense and survival leave me.

He's broken me down and made me something I never thought I'd be. I'm a slave to our desires.

I am only his.

CHAPTER 23

GIO

The night of the hit comes sooner than I thought it would.

Each day, I go to Grace and I train her. It goes slowly at first, but soon she warms up to the task. In fact, I can tell that she's enjoying it. She went from being afraid of leaving her cage to being out of it all the time. Sometimes she wears the clothes I give her, but more often than not she stays naked. I catch her drawing, reading, bathing, and she doesn't run like she used to.

She's finally submitted to me. My princess finally sees that it's better to give in than it is to fight.

Because I take care of her. I cater to her every need. It's true that she's still stuck in the room even though she doesn't want to be in there, but it's not much of a prison. She has everything she could possibly need.

And then some. At night when she's lonely, I can hear her softly begging my name. I love the sounds of her wanting me. I'll come to her then, in the middle of the dark long night, and I'll give her everything she needs. She arches her back under my touch as my lips graze her neck. I whisper in her ear, make her beg for my thick cock.

She wants her freedom. I understand that. She spent her whole life locked away and abused by her bastard father. My princess is tired of being locked away in a cage.

I told her it won't be forever, and I meant it. With each passing day, I try and figure out the best way to give her freedom. I need to find a way to keep her, to take her away from the Romano bastards. I need to convince my father to intercede on my behalf with the Romanos. I want her, and I'll have her. I don't want war over it. But if it comes to that... That's what it will have to be. A war. I'm not letting her go.

That's on my mind as I meet my father in a deserted parking lot on the edge of town. We're both wearing our usual hit clothing, black trousers with plenty of pockets filled with ammo and black turtlenecks. I have my rifle slung over my shoulder and he's strapped with two pistols and a shotgun. He grins at me as I climb out of my car.

"You ready for this, son?"

"Of course," I say. He laughs, clearly excited the way he

always is on the eve of a hit.

I have to admit that I'm excited, too. I can feel my darkness roiling inside of my mind, begging to be released. It needs to be fed the blood and begging of my enemies. I know I'll be feeding it soon. The excitement I feel is almost too much. And it's her father. He's caused her so much pain. Of all the men to wind up on my hit list, this one is personal.

"Let's go over the plan one more time," my father says, leading me over to his truck. He spreads a map of the city out on the hood and I stand over his shoulder, watching.

"The Don has a poker game every Wednesday night," he says. "It's here, on the South Side in some shit rundown deli. He thinks nobody knows about it, but I've been staking him out." I follow my father's finger as he points to the various locations.

"Okay, so he plays poker. He's guarded though." I know he is. Every video feed shows at least three men with him. Men who could turn on me the second the first bullet flies out. I don't care for shootouts. I prefer a clean hit.

"Right," he confirms. "That's where I come in. I'm going to set their cars on fire, here," he says, pointing. "Once ablaze, they'll come out. That's when you shoot him from here." He points to another spot.

"What's that?"

"It's a building across the street. Abandoned, the perfect spot."

I nod, my face tight. It seems like a decent plan, though I

don't like the uncertainty around the distraction. Still, this sort of thing has worked in the past, and I know I won't miss the shot.

"Before we do this, I want something," I say.

He leans back against his truck, raising an eyebrow. "What do you want?"

"The girl," I say.

He pauses, surprised. "You want that mafia bitch?"

"Yes." I don't like that he called her a bitch, but I let that slide. For now, at least. Until I have her, and she's safe.

"What the fuck for?"

"She's mine. I've grown... attached."

"Shit," he says, laughing. "You got pussy whipped."

I have to keep myself under control. I need his help in convincing the Romanos to let me keep her.

"She's not a good sex slave," I say. "The Romanos won't like her."

"You did it wrong, then."

"I didn't," I say fiercely. "She's just stronger than you realize."

He watches me for a moment, then sighs. "You really want her? You can have her."

I blink, surprised. I didn't think he'd give in so easily.

"Okay," I say. "You'll help me convince the Romanos?" It was his idea to begin with, and I have faith in my father. He can convince them. I know he can.

"They don't really give a fuck about her," he says. "If we pull this hit off, you can have as many Romano sluts as you want."

I clench my fist but instead of slamming it into his jaw, I just nod. "Good," I say. "Let's go then."

"Fuck yeah," he whoops. I can tell his blood is up and he's already forgotten about our conversation.

As we get into his truck and head over to our positions, that conversation is all I can think about. To my father, Grace is just some mob bitch to be used and abused until you're finished with her. She's just a wet hole to fuck and fill. But to me, she's become much, much more than that.

I'm protective of her. I'm possessive of her. I find myself wanting to be more tender, gentler, more loving than I've ever been in my entire life. When I'm in that room with Grace and she's giving herself to me, the darkness is completely silent.

Nothing silences the darkness. Or at least nothing had before, except maybe at the moment of the kill. When I'm with Grace, though, the darkness is totally quiet. There is only me and her and what we're doing, our bodies intertwined or just lying side by side afterward. She makes me feel something I'd never felt before.

She makes me feel at peace.

I glance at my father as we drive to the South Side of Chicago. He's probably never felt a moment of peace in his life. He has the darkness inside of him, too, just like I do. He probably thinks that the darkness will go away if the Romanos let him into the *familia*, but I know better.

Nothing so shallow could ever silence it. I don't know

what could help him. I doubt anything at this point. He's a lost cause, but I'm not. Grace showed me that. *My princess.*

We finally reach the spot where the hit will go down. We park down the block, and my father points out the building.

"There, on the left, is the deli," he says, pointing. "And that on the right is your building." He points at a taller brownstone building that looks like it was once a shopfront with apartments on top.

"Roof access?" I ask him.

"There's a fire escape on the back. You can get up that way."

I nod. Fire escapes are convenient and cleaner. "Timing?" I ask.

"I'll give you," he checks his watch, "ten minutes to get into position. Then the fire starts." He grins at me.

"Fine. Plenty of time." My blood pumps with adrenaline. My body tenses, knowing the time has come.

"Remember, one shot. Then we're out of here. I'll be nearby waiting in case something goes wrong."

"I understand." I open the door and climb out.

"Son," he says. I look back at him. "Don't miss."

I grin. "You know I don't."

He nods as I turn and walk quickly down the street.

The block is quiet. It's a pretty normal-looking residential street on the South Side. The buildings are large brownstones some with flowerpots on the steps, but they're all in pretty bad condition. This is the neighborhood the city forgot about, and so crime is rampant.

It doesn't surprise me that the Don comes here to play poker. The Rossis have safe houses all over this neighborhood. It's their main turf. Besides that, he grew up in this place. He probably still has friends in the old neighborhood, and I'm betting he's playing with them right now.

I check my watch as I walk toward the building. Eight minutes to go. I find an alley between the buildings and head down toward the back.

I scout around the corner, and it's completely quiet. It takes me a second before I spot the fire escape. I walk over and climb up onto a dumpster before jumping up and grabbing the lowest rung. It slides down with a metallic grind. I dangle there for a second, watching, but nobody comes outside.

I pull myself up and climb. It takes me a few minutes, but finally I crest the roof and find myself standing above the block. I check my watch one more time. Three minutes to spare.

I get into position at the edge of the roof and crouch down to set up my rifle. I have a silencer at one end, a high powered scope, and a tripod on the front. I rest the tripod on the ledge and adjust the scope until it's perfect. The distraction should separate them enough. And with the fire escape, I'll be gone before they can get to me. Just one kill. The others can do whatever the fuck they want.

My heart is beating fast. I take a few deep breaths to calm myself, holding onto my rifle. I scope out the front of the deli and it's deserted, though that doesn't mean anything. There are clearly three mafia trucks parked outside. They're the only nice cars on the block.

I hold my rifle, waiting. I've done this hundreds of times before. I'm a damn good shot, and I never miss. I've never killed a Don before, but he's a man like any other. One bullet to his skull, and he'll go down.

Seconds tick past, and then minutes. I check my watch with a frown.

He's late. Eleven minutes pass, and then twelve. There's no fire down there, hell, there's no sign of my father.

When fifteen minutes come and go, I'm beginning to worry. My blood races with anxiety. Something happened down there. He's never late like this, not on an important hit. Maybe he's a piece of shit in our daily lives but when we're out on a mission together, he's as dependable as anything else in this world. He's a fucking rock.

Not tonight. He's late for the first time in our career together. I have no clue why, or what's wrong. We didn't set up walkies. I didn't even think about them because we never use them, but of course that was a stupid decision.

I turn and look back at the roof. I'm secluded, and I realize that my only way off is the fire escape. There's no entrance to the roof from the actual building itself.

A sound catches my ear. I look around, frowning. It's a low chop, a sputtering noise. It takes me a second to identify it.

It's a helicopter, flying low, directly toward me.

Suddenly, it clicks. The spot I'm in, the phone call, my father's lateness. It all makes sense.

I grab my rifle and whirl it toward the helicopter, taking aim. I fire off two shots, but it keeps coming faster than I expected. I have to reload as it screams toward me, descending onto the roof. I curse myself for not bringing something that holds more ammo.

My father. That fucking bastard. Panic and anger rise up in me as I prepare to fire off more shots, desperately trying to defend my impossible position.

Wind whips my body. It's going to fucking land a few feet away from me, and I'm suddenly cut off from the fire escape. I wasted my chance to try to escape by shooting at them like a fucking fool. There are some bullet holes in the front glass, but the pilot seems unharmed.

Four men with high powered rifles jump out of the helicopter. They're screaming at me, but I don't hear them. I fire off two more shots, clipping one guy in the shoulder before they're only feet away from me. I drop my rifle to the ground and throw a punch at the first man that comes at me. My fist cracks into his jaw with a meaty thud. I feel satisfied for half a second until someone hits me in the back of the head and I fall forward.

My fucking father. That bastard, that son of a bitch. He set me up. I don't know why he would do this to his own son.

His own flesh and blood.

Feet smash into my body, and then I'm being dragged. Someone throws me into the helicopter and then the world is dropping away.

Blackness overwhelms me as I'm knocked unconscious from the butt of a gun slamming against my temple.

CHAPTER 24

GRACE

Gio better let me out of this damn room. I color in the sketch, shading it. I love this one. He's going to love it, too. I keep looking to the door. He's late tonight. He told me he would be, but I still don't like it.

I only get to see him. I miss... I miss variety, I think. I tried to explain it to him earlier. I need to get out of here. Soon. He always says soon. But I need a timeline. I love being his princess, his submissive, his... his everything. That's the way he makes me feel, and I love it. But I need to get out of this damn room.

I put the pencil down and hold the paper away from me. It's beautiful. In my periphery, I see the cage. It looks so small now. It's odd, how before it didn't seem to be. But I can't imagine going back in.

I turn to look toward the door as I hear Gio coming. My forehead pinches as I move to kneel for him. We always start the nights with training. It's basically foreplay for me now. I place my hands on my thighs, and my pussy clenches waiting for him. But there's something wrong. The footsteps sound... different. I jolt as something bangs on the door.

My heartbeat races with worry. *Gio?*

I hear a muffled voice, and then another. That's not Gio. My blood runs cold, and I scramble off the bed. Someone's here. The banging has stopped, but I hear them punching in a code. It won't work. Only Gio can open that door. I walk backward, my eyes on the door, wide with anxiety.

My throat closes, and I struggle to breathe. *Where's my Gio?*

I almost run to the cage, as if hiding would save me, but it won't. Nothing will save me. If these men are here, it means something bad happened to Gio. I know he wouldn't let them near me without a fight.

My chest tightens, and I look around the room for anything that can be used as a weapon. My easel. I run toward it, holding my breath. I nearly scream as a large thud on the door accompanied by shouting makes my body freeze with fear.

I crack the easel over my leg, and then split the large stick of wood into two. The edges are jagged. I hold both tightly in my hands, feeling the wood dig into my palms. I wait, moving back and forth on my heels, but I don't want to stand out here in the open. I have nowhere to hide though. I look under the bed, but it wouldn't give me much room to fight. Instead, I move to the bathroom and hide behind the tiny edge of the doorframe.

My heart races with anxiety. I close my eyes tightly, praying for Gio to come.

I cover my mouth with a sob and drop the one weapon as I realize he could be dead. My father. He's come for me! He better not have killed him. Not Gio. I can't bear the thought.

No!

No! Gio! I can't go back to my father and that wretched life. I won't. As the thought resonates through me, the door smashes open and the sound of several men coming into the room echoes off the walls. A large cloud of dust and smoke billows into the room, and I can barely make out the men. My heart sinks, and I slide down the wall, my fingers searching for the weapons I dropped in my panic.

I barely feel the tips of the wood with my fingers and I grab them with a force that nearly snaps them in two. I slide up the wall, waiting as deep voices speak in Italian. The smoke and dust is beginning to settle. Over the sound of the blood rushing in my ears, I can't make out a damn thing they're saying. Not that I'd understand, anyway.

As the footsteps come closer, I prepare to strike. At least one person is going to die. I'm not leaving. I don't want to leave.

The irony of the situation settles heavy on my shoulders. I couldn't wait to leave, but now all I want to do is stay. A shadow slowly creeps into the room.

I hold my breath, raising the stakes and as soon as the first boot lands on the tile, I turn and put all my weight into the blow.

I scream out and nearly collapse when I see who it is.

He grabs my wrist and my elbow, keeping the first stake from hitting him, but the second lands on his shoulder, slicing through the thin shirt and stabbing into his flesh.

Uncle Toni.

I scream, covering my mouth and hunching on the ground in shock and fear.

His face scrunches with agony as his piercing curse reverberates off the wall and the other men come in.

Uncle Toni rips the stake out as someone I vaguely recognize sees me and yells to someone else.

I huddle on the ground. "I'm so sorry." I heave in a breath.

The man throws me a blanket, and Uncle Toni kneels down. "Grace," he says and looks at me with such sadness in his eyes that I fall into his embrace, covered in the blanket.

I'm shocked and shaking with fear. The adrenaline and anxiety aren't even close to being gone. I start to say something. I want to rattle off questions and ask about Gio.

Does he know?

I need to know what's going on, but when I pull back to

look my uncle in the eyes, the men have all gathered around me and there's only one I recognize well. Alec. He's always by my father's side.

I can hardly breathe, and the fear must be written on my face. I can't go back.

My body is cold and numb. I'm outnumbered.

"Shh, it's alright, Grace," my uncle says, pulling me in closer. My heart beats so hard, it hurts. I want to tell him everything. I need to know what's happened. But with the cold dead eyes of that man on me, I say nothing. I let my uncle appear to comfort me.

"We've got you now." He strokes my back. "That sick fuck is dead." My knees collapse inward and crash on the cold hard tile.

"Gio?" I whisper his name.

"It's okay, Grace. He's gone. He's never going to hurt you again."

No, I shake my head, violently. My lungs refuse to fill, and I struggle to move. I'm paralyzed. No, not Gio. He can't be gone.

I try to swallow and regain some sort of composure. I have to tell him.

"Move," Alec's cold voice says, and my uncle steps aside. "I've got her," he says, leaning down to pick me up. I start to push him away, but I see flashes of my father. I can't disobey.

I tremble in his arms and stare at my cage past him and in

the other room.

He's dead. I blink away the tears. How could he leave me?

I grip onto Alec's shoulders as he carries me away, speaking to my uncle in Italian. The cage grows small, and eventually it's gone from my sight. I can hear barking outside, and part of me wonders what that is. A man walks by with scratches on his face, clutching his arm.

As I walk through his house, my heart splits in my chest, shattering into irreparable pieces. He can't be dead.

They can't take him from me.

I need him.

I won't live without him. I can't.

CHAPTER 25

GIO

The world is just motion, light, and shadow. I'm not sure where I am, or when. I'm dizzy from the blow to my skull but I'm still alive, which is a relief.

Or maybe a curse. I try to move, but I can't. My chin is in my chest and my body aches; it's stiff and sore. It takes me a minute to figure out that I'm tied to a chair. My hands are bound behind my back, zip ties cutting into my skin.

I lean my head back and groan. My entire body hurts from the multiple kicks they gave me, and probably worse. Every tiny breath hurts. Fuck, I hope my ribs aren't broken. The room slowly begins to materialize around me as I get more and more of my faculties back.

Above me there's a bright spotlight shining directly down on me. It makes me squint as I open my eyes. I can hardly see out of my left. It must be swollen. I wipe my chin against my shoulder. It's dirtied with blood.

I groan and look straight ahead as the room comes into focus. I'm in a small room, maybe ten feet by ten feet. There's a drain beneath my feet, and the walls are bare white cinder blocks. The ground looks like it's unfinished concrete.

The unbelievable nature of my reality comes back to me slowly. My fucking father sold me out. It couldn't be anything else. They knew I would be on that roof with almost no way to escape. Trapping me like that was their only option. They had to set me up like that because if they came any other way, I would've killed them all. They sent a fucking helicopter because they were too afraid to face me, the cowards.

Why would he do that? What could the Rossis possibly offer him that would change his mind? We were so close to getting what we wanted. I would have gotten Grace, and he might have gotten a place in the Romano *familia*. Instead I'm fucking strapped to a chair, aching from a hundred bruises.

Oh fuck. Grace. My heart stills, and I struggle harder in my bonds. She's still locked in the gun room without any food. Fuck, fuck, fuck. I come fully awake at the thought of Grace stuck in there, slowly starving to death, begging me to come help her. I flex against my restraints and struggle, anger flooding me, desperate to escape.

I need to go to her. *My princess.*

I have to save her. I can't let her starve to death in that room. Fuck! My selfish need to keep her is going to cause her pain. I should have let her go. I know I should have. Things were going so fucking good. She loves it. And I fucking love her. I fucking know I do. I was too scared to risk her leaving me.

At least Duke is probably okay. He has his doggy door and an auto-feeding system. I know he'll be smart enough to run if they attack my place, and he can get food and water from the feeding system. At least I didn't get him fucked, too.

My darkness is there inside of me, raging in full force. It wants revenge against my father, while all I want is to run home and make sure Grace is safe.

"Hey!" I yell out. "Fuckers! Come in here, you fucking cunts!"

There's silence as I continue to struggle. Eventually, I tip over the chair and crash to the ground, smashing my face against the concrete floor. Fuck! I stretch my bruised jaw, moving away from the cold unforgiving ground. I grunt and nearly lose consciousness, but manage to stay awake.

A minute later, the door opens. Someone comes inside. I can only see his feet as he walks over to me. My breaths come in quickly as adrenaline fuels my blood.

The man grabs me and lifts me back upright. I stare into his face, defiant and angry. I hope he fucking drops me. I hope he kicks the fucking chair. He needs to. I need this chair to break so I have a chance. I need to get to her. As the plan formulates in my mind, I realize who it is I'm staring at.

It's him. The Don, Grace's father. The man I want to kill more than anything in this world for what he did to his daughter. To my princess.

"So," he says. "You're the one that was holding my daughter."

I stare at him, not saying a word.

"You're in a pretty bad spot now, Gio," he says. "We know all about you, you know. Have known for some time."

"Go fuck yourself," I practically spit at him.

I almost tell him where Grace is. I almost do, but I'm afraid of what he'll do to her. And as sad as it sounds, my father knows she's there. He knows what she means to me. If he ever loved me, he'd save her.

"Good. Defiant. Strong. I like that about you. I can see why my daughter is interested in you."

I stare at him, but say nothing, even as fear strikes through my veins. "We found her locked away." He tsks. He's just fucking with me. He doesn't know a fucking thing about me and Grace. I can't give in to his games. There's no way he has her.

"Tell me, Gio," he says as he walks behind me. I can hear him doing something back there that sounds like clattering metal. Finally, he comes back around. He's holding a wicked, large curved knife in his hand and he has a big smile on his face. "Tell me what you know about the Romanos."

I stare at him and say nothing. The smile never leaves his face as he carves a cut into the meat of my thigh.

I grunt, seething through clenched teeth as the pain floods me, but I don't cry out. I won't give him the satisfaction.

"Talk, Gio," he says. "I wanna know everything about the Romanos and their enemies. I want names. Your father already sold you out. Your very own flesh and blood sold you out for a position in our *familia*. Can you imagine that?" I hold back the pain, even though I already knew it. It fucking hurts. He clucks his tongue and shakes his head. "Well, he won't last long with us. We don't take kindly to rats, although I do appreciate him showing me where my Grace was locked away."

I grunt and flex against my bonds, trying to get free. Anger viciously tears through my body, and I know only violence will sate that anger. I can barely breathe at the thought of my father giving her back to him. Handing her over to a man who caused her so much pain. The betrayal of that is far greater than what he did to me.

My piece of shit father. This bastard, Grace's father. Both men are dead. I'm going to tear them limb from limb until they're screaming for my mercy. I won't stop. I won't ever stop.

"Go fuck yourself," I say to him just beneath my breath.

He laughs and carves into my other leg, the sharp knife slicing easily. I wince and grunt in pain, clenching my teeth and barely falling forward, but I still don't cry out. I've had worse. I can handle this.

I'd rather die than be a fucking rat. I'll let him destroy me if I have to, but I'll never talk.

It goes on like that for a while. I don't know how long. He asks me questions, I don't answer, and then he cuts into me.

He gets creative after a while, taking thin slices and pouring salt onto the open wounds. At least that makes it numb for a while. I'm in so much pain that my vision becomes blurred. They give me breaks, even feed me and give me water, but the pain comes back.

I sleep at least once. I don't know for how long. I'm in that room, strapped to that chair, and it's all I know.

I don't say a word. I'll never talk. I can feel my life hanging in the balance, and part of me wants it to finally end.

But the other part, the stronger part, wants to survive. I want to make it through this until I get the chance to have my revenge.

I'll kill them. I'll maim them. I'll tear them into pieces. For my princess. I have to live for her. I have to save her.

That's what sustains me. Rage and violence. Even through the torture, my silence never wavering, the only thing keeping me going is the rage. I worry about Grace every second, but my revenge will be for both of us.

Without her, my life is finished. I'm okay with that. I can handle that. When I'm through, I can join her, wherever she is.

For now, though, I survive. Cuts and kicks and bruises, I survive. A day, maybe two days, I can't be sure.

I don't know what time it is when Toni appears in the room. He stands near the door, his arms crossed, a smile on his face.

"The cameras were smart," he says, as if from a distance. "But you were never going to get to me. Maybe my brother, but never to me." He laughs.

"Fuck you," I mumble. It's all I say anymore.

"Right, of course. Fuck me." He grins, and I want to kill him slowly. "I'm actually here to show you something, Gio. I think it might help you find your tongue."

I spit onto the floor and stare at him.

"Okay," he says. "I just want you to know that I hold no ill will toward you. I understand that you're just doing your job. Well, except with Grace. My lovely niece, Grace. She's wonderful, isn't she?"

I stare at him, my heart beating rapidly. I hate that he'd ever use her name. None of the Rossi family deserve her.

"You wanna see her, don't you?"

I won't give in to their tricks. It's just a stupid game they're playing.

"You're desperate to make sure she's okay. Well, I can do that for you. Would you like that?"

Yes, I want to see her. I want to make sure she's okay. But not like this. Not when I can't save her. I don't give him anything. Nothing. I'll give them all nothing. "Fuck you," I mumble.

"Grace," he says. "Come in here."

The door opens with a loud creak, and daylight filters

into the room. The Don steps through, grinning wickedly.

Followed by Grace. Her head is held low.

I feel like I'm going to pass out. My heart is hammering in my chest.

It's her. She's safe. She's alive. She lifts her head to look at me, and horror passes through her expression.

They have her. But at least she's alive. At least she has a chance.

That gives me hope. I feel new strength surge through my body at the sight of her. She's so beautiful, so perfect. I know what I have to do.

I'm going to kill them. And then I'm going to take what's mine.

CHAPTER 26

GRACE

I'm barely walking as Alec pushes me toward the room. I know what door this is. The people who come in here never leave. Maybe my father's disappointment in me not knowing a damn thing has finally led him to kill me. I don't know, and I don't care.

My uncle's outside the door, and I can't even look him in the eyes. His arms are crossed and I can feel his eyes on me, but I don't return his gaze. I can't stand the sight of any of them. All those years I thought he protected me, I was a fool.

I thought he loved me, I thought he kept me safe. I was so wrong. He did nothing but keep me quiet. Maybe he prevented the beatings, but he never saved me. Not like Gio did.

The very thought makes my heart hurt.

They killed him.

I take in a sharp breath. At least Alec's shoving against my back eases slightly as we approach the door. My uncle may have some influence, but it's not enough. Not anymore. He let them hurt me. He was proud to tell me that Gio was dead.

I hate him. I hate all of them. I haven't said a word to any of them. The only thing on my mind is how to get out of here. But I have to kill my father first. That is the only thing I'm focused on. The only thing that's kept me alive since I've been back here, locked back in my room.

He hasn't even tried to talk to me. He doesn't give a fuck.

The only company I've had is my uncle. I couldn't talk to him though. I didn't say a word as he told me they were waiting to kill him. It was all about him. Why he couldn't come to my rescue because it would have put him in danger.

I understand it. I do. But I don't care.

All the years I spent here made me weak. Gio gave me a reason for living. He gave me a strength I never knew I had.

And now he's dead.

My uncle's hand rests on my shoulder, halting me in front of the door. His hand is rough and cold. He leans forward and talks quietly, "It's going to be alright." His soft words sink in, resonating in my very being.

I look him in the eyes. "No it won't," I say, and he flinches from my simple response. "It's never been alright." Truer words have never been spoken.

My gaze is ripped away as the door flies open, revealing my father.

I don't drop my gaze. It takes everything in me not to glare at him. My hate has grown and consumed me. The wits I had before that kept me safe from his anger have all vanished. Beat me. Whip me. Humiliate me. I don't care. The last thing I do will be to put this man in his grave.

"Grace," he says, and his eyes are narrowed and his yellow teeth show through his sickening smile.

I don't respond. Instead I walk in, ignoring him and preparing for whatever it is he's going to do to me.

I only take two steps in and then I freeze. My legs go numb, and my knees threaten to buckle. I gasp, covering my mouth, my heart and body going cold. My eyes prick with tears. But I can't let them come. He's here. He's alive.

My uncle grabs my waist and keeps me upright. My body's trembling.

He's alive.

"Gio!" I call out to him, and try to run to him. He's not okay. His face is bloodied, and he has bruises and cuts all over his body.

I can't stand the sight. Every inch of my body prickles with terror, and my blood runs cold. My uncle squeezes my forearms and pulls my back into his chest. I try to elbow him in his gut. I fight him, kicking and yelling for him to let me go. I can't take my eyes away from Gio though.

"Grace," he says and his voice is full of conviction as he struggles against the binds holding him to the chair. "Don't touch her!" he screams. Just hearing his voice mends a broken piece of my soul. My voice cracks, and the words refuse to leave my lips.

I finally tear my eyes away from him and fall to my knees, my hands gripping my father's shirt. "Please! Let him go!" My heart squeezes in my chest. If he ever loved me, he'd save him. A sob rips from my throat.

"He didn't do anything, please-" The back of my father's hand whips across my face. The force of the blow is so strong it makes my head spin as I land hard against the ground.

"You fucking cunt." I open my eyes, and through my blurred vision I see Alec's cruel smile and then my father's.

My heart collapses. They'll never save him.

I repress every emotion in me other than hate. A black void starts taking over.

I can hear the screaming. Gio and my father. The legs of the chair Gio's tied to are scraping against the floor. But it all turns to white noise. My body heats and an anger I've never felt grips hold of me, bolting me to the floor as it seeps into my blood.

"You're a fucking rat!" my father hisses as he crouches closer to me, close enough to hit me again. My head flings to the side, and my lips pulse from the impact. The stinging pain shoots from my heated cheek down my throat. I anticipated it though. I only use it to fuel me and my growing rage. My tongue darts out, and the metallic taste of blood fills my senses.

"She doesn't know anything!" Gio screams. I stare at the cinder blocks on the wall, focusing on my breathing, taking in the room. Looking for options.

It's quiet for a moment as my father paces. I know he's going to kill Gio. I can't let him. I won't be able to breathe if I watch him die at the hands of my father.

I look over my shoulder. My captor, my master, my everything is so badly wounded and scarred. But he's still fighting. I won't stop fighting either. Not till the very end.

Gio's eyes are darting from me to my father, the hardness in his features replaced by a vulnerability I've never seen as he says, "Just let her go." His breathing is coming in heavy pants as my father lets out a humorless laugh. "She didn't do anything. She didn't tell me anything."

I didn't. I have nothing to tell. But the truth isn't what my father wants.

This is just another reason for him to hurt me. Maybe enough to kill me this time.

"You're my daughter. A Rossi!" He screams so loud in my face it makes my chest hurt. I flinch out of instinct, and I hate it. I scoot back on my ass, the hard concrete under my palms and watch as my father moves to the edge of the steel table on the backside of the room. His rage is consuming him like the hothead he is.

Alec moves to the side as my father grips the table and

flips it over, causing all of the knives and other weapons of torture to hurl into the air and crash onto the ground next to me. My arms cover my face as I turn my body.

Uncle Toni yells in Italian, grabbing my father by the arms and trying to keep him from beating me. Gio is screaming, his chair scooting closer and closer to me. But neither one of them can save me from the kick to my back. My father's hard boot slams into me.

"I have a rat for a daughter!" The spit from his sneer hits my face as he grips my arm and turns me toward him as he yells, "A fucking traitor!"

I see the knife. The sharp edge of it is shining in the dim light coming from the hallway. I don't hesitate to grab it, ignoring the kick to my stomach and quickly turn onto my back. It nearly slips from my sweaty palms as I grip it with both hands and reach up.

My father's eyes widen as he crouches closer, intent on beating me again.

Intent on hurting me like he's done for years. Expecting me to submit as I always have.

A violent scream rips through my throat as I plunge the blade into the side of his neck.

My heartbeat stills, and everything burns inside of me as I pull the knife out, blood gushing from his wounds and his body freezing in shock. And I stab him again, and again and again.

CHAPTER 27

GIO

The darkness in me shatters as Grace plunges the knife into her father. I'm helpless as I watch her struggle with the fear and anger and raw vulnerability shining in her eyes. Never has death seemed so real to me. And I can't do a damn thing but watch.

I struggle against the zip ties digging and cutting into the flesh of my wrists, the blood dripping down my hand from the wounds.

Fuck! I need to help her. I can't sit and watch. But I'm useless.

"You bastard!" she screams. She plunges it into his body again and again, the blade slicing through his skin.

"You bitch," he groans, finally falling against the wall as the blood spills from his neck. His hands try to stop the flow, but she's done enough damage. He's done for. He tries to fight, but he's losing so much blood too quickly.

I watch, totally helpless, unable to do a thing. I wish I could stand up and take the knife from her and finish the job myself. She doesn't need blood on her hands.

But part of me is grateful she's finally doing this. That she's the one to put an end to her pain. She's so fucking strong. I've seen this fight in her, and now she's using it. But it hurts me that she had to. I hate that it came to this. She's wanted freedom her whole life, and now she's getting it. Killing the man that locked her up and abused her for so long was one surefire way to exorcise him from her mind. He can never hurt her again, not after she stabbed him to death.

Toni stands by the door, arms outstretched. "Back off," he growls at the men that try to get past him and go to Martino's aid, even though the looks in their eyes reveal the shock, and in some of them the pride of seeing her take down her father.

Alec ignores Toni, grabbing a club that's stained with my blood from the ground. I push forward off the ground, desperate to save her from the blow, screaming and fighting again. My head smashes against the concrete, the chair landing hard in front of Grace. It's not enough, but it's all I can do. I prepare for the blow of the club to smash against my skull. Instead a loud bang ricochets off the wall. *Bang!* And then another *bang!*

My heart stills in my chest, fear crippling me. Not Grace. Please God, no.

I open my eyes and watch as Alec falls to the ground, knees first and then his upper body collapsing. His eyes are open and lifeless, a small hole in his neck bubbling blood. I watch as the blood seeps around his neck and soaks into his shirt.

"Let the girl finish this," Toni says from behind me, and I turn slightly to watch.

Grace breaks down into wordless sobs as she looks to her uncle, ignoring the cursing her father barely manages to mutter, and shoves the knife into her father's throat. With a final gurgle he's silenced forever, the blood seeping all over the concrete floor.

The blood runs down the concrete and slides into the drain underneath my chair. The Rossi Don is dead, and Grace is drenched in his blood.

Toni stares at Grace. He doesn't bother glancing at me, and I don't blame him. As far as he's concerned, I'm nothing. Toni probably never imagined Grace would have the balls to do this, but now it's done. It's something he should have done a long time ago.

And he's the leader of the Rossi family. By rights, he's the Don now.

Toni steps toward Grace. "Honey," he says softly, reaching his hand out to her. "Give me the knife." The men by the door stand and wait for their next command.

She stares up at him with tears in her eyes. "What?" she says after a long moment as if she didn't hear him.

"The knife, Grace. Give it to me."

"Give it to him," I say to her. She can't fight him, too. She can't fight the entire *familia*. He won't hurt her. None of them will. He better let her go.

She glances at me, taking in a ragged breath, then nods to herself. She hands the knife over to Toni. She needs to be held. I struggle once more, useless and feeling defeated. *She needs me.*

He takes it, then hands it off to one of his thugs. People gather at the entrance to the room, staring in at the dead body of the Don slowly bleeding on the ground. There's so much blood, and I'm betting that everyone is surprised at how much he's bleeding. I've seen it plenty of times before. The body holds a lot of blood, and it's always a shock to see it all spread out on the floor.

"That's a good girl," Toni says to her. He slowly helps her to her feet. I stare at them, not sure how I feel about this. He's being sweet to her, but I can see the shrewdness behind his eyes. He's already calculating what he can do with her and how he can use her for his own benefit. She needs to get away from all of them. They only see her as a pawn, and she's so much more than that. She deserves so much more.

"Let her go," I say to him.

His eyes flash to mine.

"I'll give you whatever you want."

He sneers at me. "What could you possibly have that I'd want?"

"I have names of contacts, the locations of warehouses."

I know saying these things makes me a rat, but I'll give him anything and everything to let her go. "I know arrangements that are being made this very minute. But you know you're not upset Grace just killed your brother. You're the Don now. You got what you wanted."

He watches me for a second, his eyes narrowing, then looks at Grace. "What do you think, Gracie dear? Do you want to leave?"

"Yes," she says in a small voice. I can tell that she's still processing what just happened, and I can't blame her. This is the first time she's taken another person's life. She's in shock.

He pulls her toward him and rubs her back. It's comforting and without any eyes on his face but my own, I can see the hurt behind his. He may be a sick fuck, a killer and someone who's willing to sacrifice her if need be, but somewhere deep down he must care for her. "Okay then." Toni looks at me. "I have an offer for you. Are you ready?"

"I'm ready," I say.

"Why do the Romanos want war?" Grace turns in his embrace, her eyes on me.

I stare at him for a second, surprised at the question. I assumed that the answer was obvious, but the truth hits me in a sudden realization.

The Rossis have no clue why the Romanos are coming at them. Maybe they have guesses, but the Romanos haven't actually contacted them. As far as they can tell, it's just a random attack without any provocation.

"It's over territory," I answer him. "You made a deal with the Zhang Syndicate that the Romanos used to do business with. They cut the Romanos off, and they're pissed."

"How the fuck is their decision my problem?" He releases Grace and she backs away, but her eyes fall to her father and then to me.

"We could have negotiated," he says with a hard voice, his jaw tensing.

"It's easier to negotiate with a dead man," I point out.

He shakes his head, clearly considering what I've said.

"Let him go," Grace says, breaking the silence.

My princess. I look at her proudly.

Toni laughs. "He really fucked you up, didn't he?"

I glare at the asshole. Anger rolls through me, but I need to play my cards right. I keep myself under control. For now.

"Okay," he says finally. "I think I have a deal for you."

"What is it?" I ask, impatient.

"Take a message to the Romanos for me. If you do that, I'll let you live. If not, I'll have my whole *familia* hunt you down. Understand?"

"What message?"

He grins. "Just a little something. I'll tell you how to find it soon. Do we have a deal?"

I stare at him, and I know I should turn this down. I shouldn't accept without knowing exactly what this message is.

But then I look at Grace, and I have to accept. She can't be given back to these people, these fucking animals. She's mine and I'll do anything in my power to keep her and keep her safe.

"I accept," I say.

"Wonderful." Toni grins huge, then gestures at me. The thug with the knife walks in and cuts away my ropes and the zip ties from around my wrists.

Slowly, I stand. My muscles groan in pain, but I don't care how sore my body is. Grace pushes off the wall and runs to me. She throws her arms around my neck and I pull her close against me, holding her tight. My eyes never leave her uncle though, or any of the other men. I don't trust them. We need to leave while we can.

I can't deny the relief of holding her in my arms though. I hurt from a million bruises and I can barely stand, but I've never felt better in my entire fucking life.

She pulls back and stands at my side, facing her uncle. "I'm leaving with Gio," she announces with a firm voice.

He raises an eyebrow. "The fuck you are. You're a Rossi."

"I'm leaving," she says. "My father is dead, and I'm free now." The men shift uncomfortably, watching the two stare each other down. I move in front of her protectively. He has no reason to keep her, but he could if he wanted to.

Toni stares at her, then looks at me. "Is this what you want, too?" I can see the resolve in his expression. An immense pressure leaves my chest.

"She goes where I go," I say simply.

He shakes his head, his expression mystified. "What a fucked up pair."

I can't help but grin. *Maybe, but I wouldn't have it any other way.*

Toni sighs. "Fucking hell. Fine, girl, go with him. I don't give a fuck. But remember, if he doesn't live up to his promise, you're both dead." His expression turns to ice.

I take Grace's hand and we walk forward without another word. I'm limping more than I'd like, but that doesn't matter. I'm going to leave this place with Grace, and she's going to know that she's free.

We head past her uncle, past the thugs in the hall, and toward a door at the far end.

"This way," she says, tugging at my hand

We walk down the hall together and push open the door.

As soon as I we get outside, I hold Grace tightly against my body, taking a moment, just a small moment to really hold her. I'm so proud of her. "You did good, princess," I whisper into her ear.

"I killed him," she says softly. I can hear the pain in her voice, but what's more, I can hear the gratification.

"I'm proud of you."

She pulls back and looks at me, raw vulnerability in her eyes. "Really?"

"Really." I kiss her softly on the lips.

CHAPTER 28

GRACE

I could feel the knife plunging into his neck. My father. The Don.

I killed him.

I've wanted to kill him for so long. I fantasized about it. I wept for hours in my room after they told me Gio was dead, imagining all the ways I'd kill him. I didn't know how I'd do it, and now that it's done, I'm still in disbelief.

I didn't hesitate. I didn't think. I just saw the chance, and I acted. I grabbed the knife and I killed him as all of the fury and rage from my whole life spilled out of me in that moment.

I felt horrible. I felt broken. And I felt ... liberated.

It felt *good*. Yet again, I feel as though I must be sick. 've killed, and I have no regrets. I've fallen in love with a man who took me prisoner. I must truly be sick.

"Princess?" Gio's rough cadence when he calls my name makes my body heat with need.

I look over, snapped out of my thoughts. Gio is looking at me, concern clear on his face. We're stopped at a red light. His truck is idling beneath us. We had to walk a few blocks, and all the while I gripped his hand with fear as though my father was coming for us. But he's dead. I have to keep reminding myself of that fact.

"I'm okay," I say softly. For some reason, I want to lie to him. I don't want him to be upset or to worry about me. I know that's crazy, but it's the truth.

"You're not okay," he says simply. "We'll be home soon." He reaches across the truck and takes my hand, a sudden and comforting gesture.

It's such a small thing, but I needed it.

Home. I've never had a home. Only a prison. I look at him from the corner of my eye and wonder if he's going to put me in that room. He can't. It will crush me if he tries. I'm finally free, and I know what I want. I want *him*. I want a life together. But I can't be caged anymore. *Never again.*

I lean back in the seat and nod my head. Gio is bruised and beaten, in horrible shape, but he's still going. He's the strongest man I've ever met. He was willing to do anything to save me, to keep me safe. Despite everything, I know the kind of man Gio is. He's the kind of man I want beside me for the rest of my life. I think he wants me too, but I need to hear him say it. I'm desperate for those words.

The image of my father's bleeding corpse keeps coming back to me.

I squeeze Gio's hand, and he squeezes back. I have to hold on tightly or else risk falling into my waking nightmare. Gio can help me. I know he can. He's been through this before. He's killed before.

We pull up to his house, the gravel driveway rumbling beneath the tires. I get a good look at it for the first time, the only time, without any fear. It's a beautiful house, built to look like a cabin, but I know it's much bigger than it seems.

It looks like a home. I can just picture the porch swing. I look to my left at Gio and I wonder if he'd build one for me. He's given me everything I've ever asked for. But things are different now.

They'll always be different.

"Come on, princess," he says as he climbs out of the truck. He walks around the front and takes my hand again. "Let's go inside."

"Okay," I say nodding my head and feeling so unsure, and let him lead me through the large front door.

I take a good look around as I enter. I vaguely remember the modern furniture and clean sleek lines as my uncle took me away a few days ago. Gio takes me into the kitchen and sits me down at the granite island on a bar stool. It feels strange to be in his house but not in my room. To be free for the first time. Even at my father's house, someone was always watching. I look up at Gio and wonder if that will be him from now on.

Something inside of me settles, knowing the answer already. Gio's different. I know he is.

It also feels normal to be sitting there with him. He goes into the refrigerator and offers me wine. He pulls a bottle out, dark purple, almost black. I can't read the label, but it doesn't matter.

"No thanks," I say in a soft voice, although I could use something for my nerves. I'm too shaken, and I feel on edge. But I need my wits. He nods and makes himself a drink. Whisky with ice. He sits down across from me, ice clinking in his glass.

We're quiet for a moment as I take in the place.

"Come here," he says, holding an arm out.

I stand quickly, needing his touch. I need his comfort; I need his reassurance. He reaches out and grabs my hips, pulling me toward him and into his lap. I bury my head into his chest, loving his warmth as he holds me there. I curl up against him and for the second time, I let myself go.

I sob into his chest. Everything seems to be too much for me to handle anymore.

He holds me, softly stroking my hair. "It's okay," he

says softly.

But it's not okay. I killed my father. I murdered him with a knife in the most brutal way imaginable. There was so much blood, so much more than I could have imagined. I still can hardly believe that I did it.

I'm a sobbing, shaking mess, my body trembling and my breath coming in ragged, but Gio holds me tight and whispers gently into my ear. "It's okay, it's okay. I have you. I'll never let you go, princess."

That's what I need to hear. Never let me go. I can't live without him.

After a good hard sob, I'm an exhausted wreck. He releases me as I finally calm down. He wipes my tears and kisses my cheeks.

"You're safe now, princess," he says.

I shake my head, not feeling safe or secure at all. I wrap my arms around myself and take in a long inhale, just trying to calm down

"Trust me." He pauses and looks me in the eye. "You trust me, don't you?"

"Of course," I say softly.

I climb off his lap after a few minutes and pace across the kitchen. It's a large kitchen with a big island in the middle. The tile backsplash is a blue and green geometric pattern, and the cabinets are all dark wood. The appliances are stainless steel. It looks like a normal home. Like a real home.

"Can I have a tour?" I ask, trying to keep my mind off the images. The horrible images that keep flooding through my mind

"Of course. You can do whatever you want, princess."

I smile, then walk out of the kitchen. He follows me, drink in his hand, ice clinking against the glass.

His living room is sparse, but nicely furnished. There's a lot of light from multiple large windows and a sliding glass door in the back. I walk through the living room and he lingers behind me, not saying anything. He lets me wander around his home, looking at every little thing. I'm not taking it in though. I'm only distracting myself, and I'm sure Gio knows that. He's patient though.

I look into his bedroom, at his large bed. There are guns stacked in the corner.

The bed looks so inviting. I strip out of my clothes and crawl onto it, pulling the covers over my body. I look back at Gio, wanting to see his reaction.

I can't go back to the room. I just can't.

Gio gives me a small chuckle as he walks over to the bedside. "You can't sleep in the middle. I need room, too." He leans down and kisses my forehead, pushing the hair from my forehead.

A sense of relief washes over me, but it doesn't last long.

"We have to go, princess."

I look at him with a hint of worry, pulling the blanket

closer to me. I don't want to leave. I just want to stay here and deal with everything threatening to consume me. I'm overwhelmed.

"I have to go see my father." It takes a moment for his words to sink in. I know his father's the one who sold him out. Tears prick at my eyes, but the anger keeps them away. "And you need to go to the safe house."

"And by 'see' you mean?" I ask with my eyes on the back wall, and a white-knuckled grip on the blanket.

"I'm going to kill him, princess. I'm going to kill him for what he did to you." Gio's voice is low and threatening.

"Don't leave me," I whisper. I feel weak, but I don't want to be left alone.

"I have to do this."

I look up at him, pleading, "Then take me with you." I don't know why I asked. It sounds ridiculous, but the thought of him leaving shreds me.

"I can't risk you. I can't."

"I don't want you to go." Tears stream down my face and I grip on to him.

He kneels on the bed and cups my chin in his hand. "My princess, I'll be back. I promise you. Let me take you to a safe place. I'll give you a phone, it's untraceable, but I'll know where you are and I'll call you as soon as it's done."

My chest pains, clenching in agony. "Please don't." The wretched words leave my lips even though I know he's going to go. There's no stopping him. This must be done.

He crawls closer to me, the bed groaning from his weight and he holds me close.

I can't resist the urge to take his lips with mine.

I pull him closer to me, gripping onto him, not wanting him to leave.

"Princess," he breathes the word, pressing his lips to mine, his tongue slipping along the seam of my lips until I part for him.

He groans into my mouth, pushing the covers away and letting his hands roam over my body.

We're both covered in blood and filth. But I don't care. I want him. I need him. I have to have him close to me, consuming every part of me.

"Don't leave me," I plead with him. Breaking the kiss only to help him strip his shirt off.

"Once more," he says, letting the shirt fall to the floor. His chest is bloodied and bruised, and it makes my heart clench with pain. I close my eyes and listen to his words as he adds, "And then never again."

He slowly lowers me to the bed, kicking his jeans off. When I open my eyes, I see his piercing gaze, full of devotion and so much more. Love. I know he does. But I need to hear him say it.

He pushes my legs wider, his hips butting against mine as he lines the head of his dick up at my entrance.

He eases himself slowly into me, moving back and forth, inching his way in. My neck arches, and my nails dig into his back.

I gasp, only then realizing that I'd been holding my breath as he slams deep inside of me, buried to the hilt.

Yes!

I need to feel all of him. Every inch of my skin comes to life as he moves in and out of me with a relentless pace. The headboard knocks against the wall as my head thrashes.

Gio grabs my chin and molds my lips to his, kissing me with the passion I have for him.

My heels dig into his ass, wanting more. I want the beast that's taken me, I need him now.

"No," Gio says, pulling away from me, but not stopping his merciless pace. "I need you like this. Raw and vulnerable and with me," he kisses me hard and with a desire that I can't deny. "Just like this." He pushes himself all the way in and pulls out slowly, taking his time and driving my release further and further up.

"Gio," I whisper as he kisses along my neck. My body heats and sweet desire stirs low in my belly, threatening to shove me over the cliff.

"I love you," I whisper the words as my back arches and my hardened nipples rub against his chest. The sensitive skin is directly connected to my throbbing clit and it brings me that much closer.

"I love you, Grace," Gio says, sucking in a breath and pounding harder and faster into me. His blue gaze pierces into me. "I love you so fucking much."

His blunt fingernails dig into my hips as he thrusts his thick cock into me over and over. A cry of pleasure tears through my throat as every nerve ending in my body blazes with a pleasure so intense I can barely stand it.

His eyes never leave mine as he rides through my orgasm, once, twice, a third time, before slamming into me and cumming with me.

We both lay in bed, panting and sated, clinging to each other. I hold onto him, every inch of my skin that I can manage touching his, not wanting to let go. I don't want him to leave me.

I'm afraid he'll never come back.

CHAPTER 29

GIO

I drive slowly up my father's winding driveway, my mind completely focused on the task at hand. I know Grace is safe back at my safe house and nobody is going to come for her. Not a soul knows where it is. I don't know why I trust the Rossis to keep their end of the bargain, but Toni doesn't have any reason to go back on his word. And I know his niece has to mean something to him. She better. He'd be a fool not to want what's best for her.

He's the Don now, and as the Don he has to live up to some level of respect. If he goes back on the very first deal he made as Don, it would set a bad fucking precedent for the rest of his time in control.

I take a deep breath, getting my mind right. My father lives in a trailer at the end of a long dirt road. He bought several acres of land a few years ago and set up his trailer there, mirroring what I did on the opposite side of town. Except where I built a gorgeous house, he just kept his old shitty trailer and hoarded his cash.

Anger rules me, but I have to keep it at bay. My father betrayed me, went behind my back and nearly got me killed. Worse than that, he put Grace in danger. He gave her back to the man who made her life hell for all those years. Grace was forced to murder her own father and could have been put into an even worse position if she hadn't. All because my father was stupid enough to think the Rossis would have him. His greed. He's going to die because of it.

His time is over. He was strong for so long, and kept his shit together well. He built our business from the ground up all on his own. But now he's finished.

He went too far. He's my father and I'm supposed to love him, but I hate that piece of shit. I've always hated him, even as a little kid. We worked well together and he took care of me, taught me his trade, and made me the man I am today, but I despised him. Because of him, the darkness ruled my life, pushed me to do things I wouldn't normally do.

But it doesn't rule me anymore. That much has become clear to me. The darkness is silent as I put the car in park and stare at the trailer. Part of me is afraid that it's just biding its time, waiting for the perfect time to come back to the surface, but I can't live my life assuming that will happen.

I have Grace now. I have my princess. Watching her in danger, knowing I couldn't save her, it destroyed that part of me. It shattered its very existence. She's the cure I've needed all my life. And I'll never let her go. I know I need her, although I don't know why. It has something to do with my desire to take care of her, to bathe her, feed her, clothe her, and to give her pleasure. I finally have a reason to exist outside of my own desires. I have someone else to satisfy now.

I pull up outside of his trailer and park just across from his door. His truck is in its usual spot to the right, so I know he's home. I slowly climb out of the truck, a shotgun slung over my shoulder.

"Bruno," I call out. "Come outside."

There's silence from the trailer. I can imagine what he's thinking. He's probably watching me, shocked, not sure what to do. He knows why I'm here, but I don't know what he's going to choose.

"Bruno," I yell again. "Come face me. Come face the son you left for dead."

Slowly, the front door opens. My father steps out, his boot heavy on the ground, his eyes haunted as he stares at me.

He's visibly drunk. I bring the shotgun down into my hands and point it at his chest. He stumbles down off the bottom step wearing a beer-stained white wife beater and torn jeans. His eyes are red-rimmed and bleary as he steps toward me, his head cocked.

Fucking hell. He's been on a bender, that's for sure. Probably since the second I got taken. Maybe that should make me feel better, that my father does have some humanity left inside of him however buried, but it doesn't. I don't give a fuck about what's left of this husk of a man I once looked up to.

"How?" he croaks.

"You underestimated me," I say.

"No," he whispers. "I didn't."

"You did. You left me for dead. You sold me to the Rossis. But unfortunately for you, the Rossis made a different deal."

"Gio," he says, stepping toward me. "My son. I never sold you out. Never."

"Liar," I say in a strong, even voice that doesn't reflect what I'm feeling. Doubt is creeping in. I want to believe him, but I know he's lying

"How could I do that?" he asks. "You're my son, my flesh and blood. Please son, you have to believe me. I never would do that. Never."

"Liar," I say again, my finger steady on the trigger.

He comes closer and closer. I don't move the shotgun. Finally, the barrel is directly against his chest and he takes his hands, wrapping them around the barrel. He stares at me, his eyes wide, and I think I can see tears starting to form

He speaks with his forehead pinched. "I raised you. I

taught you everything I know. I turned you into a man."

"You destroyed me," I say.

His eyes go wide as he understands what I'm about to do. I feel hollow, nothing but empty, and the darkness isn't there. I expected it to be, but it never appears. No anger, no emotion but an empty void. He's nothing to me. This is nothing to me.

"Goodbye, father," I say beneath my breath.

"Son--" The smile slips from his face.

I pull the trigger. The shotgun explodes into his chest, forcing him back. Blood splatters in all directions as his chest caves in. He slams to the ground with a single gasp, and then he lies still.

I walk over to his body, press the gun against his heart, and fire again. Just to make sure that bastard's dead.

I stand over my father's bleeding corpse and stare at his lifeless eyes. In all my years with him, I never once imagined it would end up like this. I always thought we'd die on a hit or rot away in prison. Never once did I think I would kill him. I never imagined I could betray him.

That changed when he betrayed me. He was dead as soon as he made that decision. Or maybe it happened sooner than that. Maybe Grace showed me what it means to be a real man, to stand up for what you believe in, to protect things you care about. Before I lived for cash and hits and that was it. But now I live for her.

My father would have gotten in the way of that. He never would have stopped trying to destroy me. And so he's dead now, the way he wanted it to happen.

I walk over to the truck and toss the shotgun in the back. I get out my large bowie knife and a roll of plastic sheeting. I walk over to my father's body and stand over him, taking a deep breath.

It's time to finish this.

I bend over him and do my work.

Several hours later, I find myself driving through the dusk hours as I head out to the Romanos main compound. I don't bother calling ahead because I know I won't be welcome either way. I'd rather this visit be a surprise than anything else. And to get it over with now, before I go back to my princess. I know she's worried, and I have the phone in my hand. But I can't call her yet. Not until this is done.

The Romanos often gather in a large Victorian house sitting on two acres to the north outside of the city. It's a beautiful little estate, probably owned by some fucking rich asshole back in the day, but now it's used as the center of one of the most powerful mafias on this side of the coast.

I pull up to the front gate and stop. A man holding a rifle stares at me as I lower my window.

"Gio, here to see Marco," I say.

"Who?" the man asks.

"Gio. Tell Marco that I have something for him from my

father. It's important."

The man stares at me, then nods. He goes to his radio and calls up to the main house. After a short conversation, he heads back over to me.

"Marco says to come up."

I nod at the man as he opens up the gate. I drive up the path and park my truck out front. More men holding weapons hang around the front. They eye me suspiciously, but I don't care. I grab the plastic-wrapped bag next to me and hop out of the car.

"Hold on," a thug says. "Gotta check you for weapons."

"By all means." I grin at him as he pats me down. When he's finished, he gestures at the bag.

"That too," he says.

I open it for him. He recoils at what's inside.

"Anything else?" I ask.

"Uh, shit, no." He's clearly shaken, and has a look of disgust on his face.

"Thanks." I walk past him and into the front of the house.

Marco is waiting for me in the kitchen. Several of his men are scattered around the large room, and I can smell something cooking on the stove. It's probably some kind of tomato sauce and pasta, if I had to guess. It's a cliché, but pasta is easy as hell when it comes to feeding large numbers.

"Gio," Marco says, standing. "What a pleasure."

"Marco." We don't shake hands. He looks at me with a

smile on his face, but I know there's menace behind everything he does.

"To what do I owe this pleasure?" he asks.

"I have a message for you from the Rossis."

His face darkens, and the smile disappears. "Since when do you work for them?"

"I don't," I say. "But he did."

I open the bag and dump my father's severed head out onto the table.

The men all take a step back except for Marco, who stands his ground without changing his expression in the least. Marco stares at the head with a shocked silence surrounding us, his men waiting for orders.

Fucking pussies. For a bunch of hardened criminals, they sure do act like a bunch of babies over one severed head.

"That's your father," Marco says at last.

"That's right. We were going to hit the Rossi Don, but my father sold me out instead." He clucks his tongue and takes a step back, narrowing his eyes and considering my words.

"How did... this happen?" he asks, gesturing at the head.

"The Rossis made a new deal with me. The old Don, Martino, is dead. His daughter killed him, and Toni is in charge now. Toni's offer for peace is that if I killed my father and brought you his head, we'd be square." I shrug and nod at the head. "That's what I've done."

"Why?" he asks, dumbfounded. "Why the fuck would he

want that?"

"My father was a piece of shit. I think he's trying to tell you that the war is only going to get worse from here on out." I shrug. "I don't know, and I don't care."

"Why would you do this to your own father?" Marco stares at me, shaking his head and looking at me like I'm a rat, like I'm the piece of shit here. It pisses me off.

"You know him. He was a scumbag. You were never going to let him in." I begin to walk backward toward the door. "He betrayed me, and he paid for it. Now we're finished."

"Wait," he says.

"No. I'm finished with you, Marco. I'm finished with the Rossis, too. You're going to let me leave this place and never come back."

"Why would I let you leave?" he asks. "How do I know this isn't a trick?"

"You know me, Marco. If I wanted you dead, you'd be dead." I pause and smile at him. "Good luck with the war."

Without another word, I turn and leave the room. My back is to him to let him know he's no threat to me. My blood runs cold knowing they could kill me. But it would break code. There would be no honor in my murder.

My job is finished. Marco doesn't say anything as I leave and head back out front. Nobody comes after me, and nobody stops me as I get into my car and drive back toward the main road.

The gate shuts behind me, and I feel slight relief. But I

won't be complete until I have my Grace in my arms.

I roll down my window and feel the cool breeze on my face. I feel free for the first time in my entire life. My father's dead, and my ties with the mafia are officially severed. The Romanos won't want me back, and the Rossis will probably kill me if they ever see me again. But as long as we stay away, they have no reason to come after us.

It's just me and Grace now. I'm nobody's fucking lapdog anymore. No more contracts from them, and no more killings. My life is in my own hands.

And the only thing I want is my princess. She's the only thing that matters anymore.

My heart hammers in my chest as I speed back toward her. I grab my phone on the passenger seat and dial up her number. The darkness is nowhere to be seen, and I feel optimistic for the first time in my life. I believe the darkness is gone, or at least it's buried down deep beneath this new feeling.

I can't wait to get back home. I can't wait to tell Grace everything. I want her to know how free I am. I want her to know how I feel about her. She's mine, she's completely mine, and she always will be.

I press down the accelerator and speed toward her, feeling light and ready.

She answers on the first ring. "Gio?" Her voice is low and full of worry.

"I'm coming, princess. I'll be there soon."

Epilogue

Gio

I step out onto the balcony and take a deep breath of the fresh sea air. I raise the coffee cup to my lips and sip the fresh, strong French coffee as the city unfolds in front of me. Duke is curled up in the corner under the small table, dozing in the morning breeze. He's gotten lazier since we moved, just like a proper French dog.

It's a beautiful town, Saint-Tropez. Situated in the south of France between Cannes and Marseille, it's a small place that's not jam-packed with tourists. It's absolutely breathtaking, just like most of southern France, with gorgeous pastel-colored homes and a sprawling view of a deep blue ocean.

Grace picked it out. Out of everywhere in the world, she

wanted to come here. It's our home now. And she loves it. That's all that matters to me. I don't remember how long it's been. Two months, maybe three. Time doesn't really matter anymore. Life is slow in Saint Tropez, which is exactly what I wanted.

I don't kill anymore. Ever since leaving Chicago, the cravings disappeared. The darkness never appears anymore, not even in my worst moments.

I take another deep breath, feeling calm and content for the first time ever.

I turn around and look into our bedroom. Grace props herself up on one elbow, smiling at me. The breeze from the open doors blows her hair out of her face. She's goddamn beautiful. I'm a lucky man.

"You're up early," she says with a yawn.

I walk in and kiss her gently on the lips. "I wanted to get your breakfast together."

"You're spoiling me." She laughs.

I shrug, smiling. "You're damn right I am. You're my princess."

"What's on the agenda for today then?" she asks, stretching her arms above her head.

"Whatever you want. I thought we might walk down to the market, get something for lunch and dinner, and then walk along the beach. Maybe stop for a drink somewhere."

"So, what we did yesterday?"

I grin. "Exactly. I also thought we could visit that little

private outcropping of rocks... "

She laughs. "You dirty man. You're just trying to get into my panties again." She rests her head on the pillow and looks up at me as though she's innocent. She's just as dirty as I am. And she knows it.

"Damn right I am." I kiss her rough on the lips as the memory of fucking her on that public beach the day before comes back to me.

After everything went down, I picked up Grace and Duke from my house, packed some bags, and we left that night. We drove around the States for a while, living off my cash, until one day we met a guy that made fake passports in Philadelphia.

From there, we flew into London. We traveled around there for a while before heading into Germany. We hit up Italy, Spain, northern France, and finally settled in Saint-Tropez.

I ended up buying this apartment, and for the first time since we left my house, we settled into a normal daily life.

Well, normal enough. I still have a shitload of money saved up, which means neither of us are going to have to work for a very long time. If ever.

For her part, I can tell Grace is the happiest she's ever been. I made sure she got to visit everything she wanted and see and do everything possible. She had so many experiences to catch up on, and I loved watching her find herself in the world.

She's free. She's my princess, but she's free. She can leave at any time if she wants, but I know she never will.

Not when we're so stupid happy together. Not when it feels like we finally make each other complete, and the horrors of our past no longer matter.

I'm going to treat her like the princess she is for the rest of her life. She'll never work a day in her life if she doesn't want to. Or she can do any job she wants. It doesn't matter to me, so long as she spoiled, pampered, and happy.

That's my life now, and it's more fulfilling than anything else. We eat, sleep, fuck, and I take care of her. That's the way life should be.

"You shouldn't let me sleep in," she says finally, sitting up and taking a look around the room.

"You need rest now. You know that."

She sighs. "Just because I'm pregnant doesn't mean I'm incapacitated."

I laugh. "Sure it does. You have to let me take care of you."

"You already do." The soft smile that plays on her lips makes my heart clench.

I glance down at the ring on her finger. The wedding ceremony happened in Spain at an ancient church on the coast. We didn't speak a word of Spanish, but it was beautiful and perfect and most importantly, it made her happy. One look at the church, and she knew she wanted it to happen there. So I made it happen.

She sighs and stretches again. I walk over to the table and pour her some orange juice. She accepts the glass gratefully.

"You're still going to love me when I'm big and fat, right?"

I smirk at her. "You'll never be big and fat."

"Correct answer."

I crawl into bed next to her and kiss her neck. "You know, princess, we could always stay in."

"Oh, can we?" She smiles at me, a little mischievous. "And why would we do that?"

"You need your rest."

"You're not going to let me rest, and you know it."

"True. I'm a bad liar."

She laughs at my joke, and sets the orange juice down on the nightstand. I take my chance to crawl on top of her.

I kiss her full and deep, joy welling up inside of me. Soon, we'll be a proper family. I'll raise my son to love and respect people, and I won't let him have the life we had.

All that matters is that Grace can find herself and we can live together, peacefully, loving, a family in paradise. Her French is wonderful, and I'm getting better. Soon we'll be proper French citizens with little French babies.

I never imagined that in my whole life. But I couldn't be happier.

With Grace and our baby, I'm more content than I could possibly imagine. The ocean stretches out into the distance and I have her, my princess, my love, the only thing that keeps me going. I'll take care of her until my heart stops beating, and forever after that.

About the Authors

Thank you so much for reading our romantic suspense. We hope you loved the book as much as we do!

More by Willow Winters
www.willowwinterswrites.com/books

More by B.B. Hamel
https://bbhamel.com/

www.ingramcontent.com/pod-product-compliance
Ingram Content Group UK Ltd.
Pitfield, Milton Keynes, MK11 3LW, UK
UKHW042044240925
8069UKWH00002B/102